The Black West
in Story and Song

Text by Michael Patrick

Songs by Cecil Williams

Illustrations by Keith Conaway

Black West Publishing

Rolla, MO 65401 and Fairhope, AL 36532

Copyright 2006 by Williams, Conaway and Patrick

All rights reserved including the right of reproduction in whole or in part in any form.

Manufactured in the United States of America

ISBN: 1-4116-7603-3
ISBN-13: 978-1-4116-7603-9

Table of Contents

Introduction: They Don't Tell 1

Explorers 13
    Estaban 13
    York 21
    James Beckwourth 29

Outlaws and Lawmen 37
    Cherokee Bill 37
    The Rufus Buck Gang 45
    Bass Reaves 51

Cavalrymen, Foot Soldiers, and Scouts 57
    The Buffalo Soldiers 57
    The Black Seminole Indian Scouts 71

Cowboys, Ranchers, and Riders 81
    80 John Wallace 81
    Bose Ikard: From Slave to Trail Drive Banker 91
    Nat Love, Deadwood Dick 97
    Isom Dart, the Black Fox 107
    Ben Hodges 113
    Bill Pickett 119
    Nolle Smith 129

Town Founders, Townspeople, and Homesteaders 135
    Benjamin "Pap" Singleton 135
    Mary Fields, Stagecoach Mary 145
    Lt. Henry Flipper and 151
    Colonel Allen Allensworth 151
    George Washington Bush 159

Bibliography - The Black West in Story and Song 165
    Biographical Sketch: Cecil Williams 169
    Biographical Sketch: Keith Conaway 170
    Biographical Sketch: Michael Patrick 171

Dedication

All books require the efforts of many people before they are published. The authors wish to acknowledge the heroic contributions of the explorers, mountain men, homesteaders, cattlemen, soldiers, and town founders who made this book possible. Certainly this book would not be possible without the historians, scholars, and writers who came before us.

On a personal level, the authors wish to recognize those who inspired us over the years.

Cecil Williams dedicates the songs in this book to his wife of 51 years, Velma Ruth Williams.

Michael Patrick dedicates the text in this book to his father, Roosevelt "Pat" Patrick, on the centenary of his birth; to his daughters, Kathryn and Shannon, and to his wife, Sheena.

Keith Conaway dedicates the drawings in this book to his father, William Martin Conaway, to thank him for the love, direction, and encouragement he gave him. Most of all, he thanks him for his sense of humor that eased the burdens and stressful moments of life. He loves and misses him very much.

Ben Hodges
Cherokee Bill
Bill
Pickett
George Bongo
The
BLACK
COWBOY
A.L. Walker

Introduction:
They Don't Tell

Most interpretations of the history, folklore, and culture of the West have followed the frontier theory of Frederick Jackson Turner. His theory emphasizes that freedom-seeking, white, Anglo-Saxon men brought civilization to the uncivilized.

American popular culture through pulp novels early in the century, the motion picture industry and the studio system continued that myth. Recently, television and even more sophisticated writers of fiction such as Louis L'Amour have seized upon Jackson's theory. In popular American culture the white frontier hero stands heroically alone against all odds to defeat the elements of evil, or anti-white values.

Obviously, in this interpretation, the Indian was the villain. The frontier wars against the Native Americans were won because of white racial superiority. Even more recently, writers such as Mari Sandoz, Dee Brown, Scott Momaday, Thomas Berger, and Larry McMurtry have reinterpreted the exploration of the West. Motion pictures, such as "Cheyenne Autumn," "The Man Who Shot Liberty Valance," "Little Big Man," "Dances With Wolves," and "The Unforgiven" have examined the reality of western myth and folklore.

Still historians and writers have largely neglected the role of African-Americans in settling the frontier. In reality, the Buffalo Soldiers (the black Ninth and Tenth Cavalry and the Twenty-fourth and Twenty-fifth Infantry regiments) comprised twenty per cent of the troops of the Missouri Department of the Army. Freedmen and women homesteaded many frontier towns, particularly in Kansas and Oklahoma. In fact, blacks were among the first homesteaders in Oklahoma when they came as slaves and freed people on the

The Black West in Story and Song

Trail of Tears in 1839 with the Cherokees, Seminoles, Creeks, Choctaws, and Chickasaws. John Ehle in *The Trail of Tears* wrote of their suffering with the Indians:

> *Few died of causes other than disease. The Trail of Tears, or as the Indians more often said, the Trail where they wept--was a trail of sickness with Indian sorcerers as doctors. Yes, and African voodoo doctors, too. The blacks' guts, too, were extended and raw, their hearts broken. One must pity them. They and the Cherokees, the Choctaws and Creeks, all walking into history, which is owned by us all (384).*

Also even though the Gold Rush of 1849 occurred before emancipation, African-Americans were quite prominent in mining in the West. In 1850 there were only about sixty blacks in Oregon. In California there were over one thousand. Many were brought to California as slaves of whites just as those who had come to Oklahoma with the Indians.

Some, such as Alvin Coffey, won their freedom through hard work in the gold fields. Daniel Rogers' white master cheated Rogers out of his freedom. Whites in his native Arkansas bought him free and gave him a certificate extolling his "honesty, industry, and integrity" (Katz, *Eyewitness*, 76).

In the folklore of the California gold mining camps, African-Americans had the reputation of being able to find gold more easily than people of other races are. So although they were usually slaves and always discriminated against, white miners often welcomed them in the camps.

Black soldiers, in addition to the Buffalo Soldiers, served with courage throughout the West, fighting the Indians and bringing peace in the range wars. General George Armstrong Custer specifically requested that Isaiah Dorman be assigned to his command as an interpreter only a month before the Battle at Little Bighorn. Dorman was not scalped and mutilated as the other white soldiers after the battle, perhaps because he was part Sioux. The Seminole Scouts never lost a man in battles with the Indians in bringing peace to the Texas frontier in an eleven-year campaign against outlaws and Indians.

Introduction: They Don't Tell

Just as significantly, popular culture and folklore have ignored or forgotten that blacks were among the first of the American mythological heroes of the West--the explorers, the mountain men and the cowboys. The most famous of these is York, who played a central role in the Lewis and Clark expedition.

Historians often have euphemistically referred to him as William Clark's "man-servant." He was born a slave in the Clark family and was approximately the same age as Clark. He grew up with Clark and remained his slave throughout his life. Professional scholars, beginning with the Reconstruction Period to the recent past, have consistently understated his role in the expedition.

After the Civil War, the southern interpretation of the Lost Cause dominated western folklore and mythology. The gallantry of the Anglo-Saxon cavalier and the Lost Cause of the Confederacy were transplanted to the frontier. Owen Wister in *The Virginian* illustrates this myth quite well.

York did not experience the almost total neglect of James P. Beckwourth, who was among the first mountain men. His native St. Louis honors other fur trappers and explorers such as Laclede, Fremont, and Chouteau with place names and monuments. Beckwourth is almost forgotten in that city. The West itself has been more kind in recognizing his discovery of a pass in the Sierra Nevada northwest of Reno. That pass, the mountain, valley, and town nearby and a street and a church in Denver bear his name. His exploits were as significant as his friends Kit Carson, Jim Bridger, and John C. Fremont were. Today, for most Americans he is unknown and is not in the pantheon of heroes of the American West.

In that pantheon of western heroes is the cowboy as an archetypal Anglo-Saxon figure even though forty per cent of the trail drivers and famous rodeo riders were either of African or Spanish heritages. Many of these black cowboys became ranchers such as Daniel Webster Wallace, better known in Texas as 80 John Wallace, who owned twelve and half sections of unmortgaged land in West Texas.

Others cowboyed all their lives. Bill Williams was a black Texas cowboy who had come to Wyoming on a trail drive and stayed to work on Lincoln Lang's ranch. He taught greenhorn rancher Theodore Roosevelt to break horses. Boise Ikard was Charles Goodnight's best hand. As Goodnight said, "He was my detective, banker, and everything else in Colorado, New Mexico, and the other wild country we traveled together" (Drotning 134).

Will Rogers learned roping from Henry Clay, a black cowboy on the 101 Ranch. Henry Beckwith was known in Texas as the best cowhand who ever lived because he could track cattle through thorny thickets and live off the land with just a blanket and a horse. Some black cowboys such as Nat Love (Deadwood Dick) were anglicized in popular culture into daredevil white heroes in early examples of pulp fiction.

The greatest of the rodeo riders, Bill Pickett, is honored in the Cowboy Hall of Fame in Oklahoma City, but almost forgotten by western historians, writers, and folklorists. Pickett was one of Will Rogers' mentors when he was a working cowboy at the 101 Ranch in Oklahoma and then when they rode together in Zack Miller's rodeo. Miller called Pickett, "the greatest sweat and dirt cowhand that ever lived--bar none."

Pickett invented, or at least refined bulldogging, a standard contest event at rodeos today. Tom Mix and Rogers, both unknowns then, assisted him in the event in the 101 Ranch shows by hazing, or riding beside the steer and swinging a rope to keep the animal running in a straight line. Mix and Rogers went on to fame and fortune in American popular culture in motion pictures and radio. Pickett continued as a working cowboy until his death at seventy-one in 1932. He was kicked by a horse on his 160-acre ranch in Oklahoma and died of a fractured skull.

Even in the 20th century reinterpretation of the Johnson County, Wyoming, range wars, the black cowboys there, such as Isom Dart, have been forgotten. Owen Wister in *The Virginian* showed his faith in capitalism in siding with the ranchers in that war. He also showed his racism in making Medicine Bow almost entirely a white community with only a few stray Indians and black cooks and servants. The Virginian is a displaced southern aristocrat who brings law, order, and nobility to the frontier. No act of the Virginian's comes close to the nobility and heroism of Isom Dart.

Arrested as a rustler in Sweetwater County, Wyoming, he was being transported to jail when the buckboard in which he and the deputy rode ran off the trail, overturned, injuring the deputy. Dart, unhurt, caught the horse, lifted the buckboard upright, and drove the deputy to the hospital at Rock Springs,

Introduction: They Don't Tell

Wyoming. There he left the buckboard at the stables and turned himself in to the sheriff. For his acts of heroism and honesty, he was presumed innocent and released from jail shortly thereafter.

After that, because of his reputation as a cattle rustler, he received, along with a number of other men and women, both black and white, a note from the Cattlemen's Association ordering him to clear out of the territory or face the consequences. Dart was found shot in the back a short time later, presumably one of the victims of Tom Horn, who had been hired by the Cattlemen's Association to rid the territory of rustlers by any means possible. Very often those whom the Cattlemen's Association called rustlers were small ranchers who added unbranded mavericks to their herds. Or they were cowboys, such as Dart. The big ranchers blackballed or wouldn't hire cowboys who ran their own cattle on the open range.

Recent novels and motion pictures have attempted to make Horn into a simple man who as an Indian scout had heroically negotiated with Geronimo to surrender. He then served the cause of law and order as a range detective. In most accounts of his role in the surrender of the Apaches, there is no mention of the Buffalo Soldiers of the Ninth Cavalry.

These black soldiers kept tracking and pursuing Geronimo until he and his band were forced, from fatigue and hunger, to surrender. All evidence indicates that Horn was the back-shooter he was hanged for being. But Horn was white and has been portrayed by such handsome actors as Steve McQueen and David Carridine as a motion picture hero betrayed by his range bosses. Isom Dart has yet to be portrayed in motion pictures.

In recent years there have been a few scattered attempts to represent black western heroes in motion pictures and television. In 1960, John Ford directed Woody Strode in "Sergeant Rutledge," the story of a black noncommissioned officer of the Buffalo Soldiers accused of rape and murder. One of John Wayne's last pictures, "The Cowboys,"(1972) stars Roscoe Lee Brown as the cook who leads the adolescent trail drivers after Wayne is killed. A few black actors such as James Brown, Richard Roundtree, Woody Strode, Ossie Davis, and Morgan Freeman have been given roles in western motion pictures starring white heroes. But, thus far, in motion pictures, and in other forms of popular culture, real heroes of the black American West have been ignored.

The Black West in Story and Song

Television has not done much better. At the height of the westerns on television, only one series, "Rawhide," had a regular black character played by Raymond St. Jacques. In the mini-series based on Larry McMurtry's novel, *Lonesome Dove*, the black actor Danny Glover played Deets, the most heroic of the drovers on the first trail drive to Montana. McMurtry probably based his fictitious hero on the Boise Ikard, whom Charles Goodnight said, "There was a dignity, a cleanliness, and a reliability about him that was wonderful."

Black women were very much a part of the settling of the West. Hundreds of black frontier women have been forgotten because settling in sod houses to raise a family and farm was not as romantic and glamorous as exploring, soldiering, or cow punching to the makers of popular culture.

Clara Brown was one of the first women to settle in Central City, Colorado, when she was sixty. She started a laundry to wash the miners' clothes. By the time the Civil War started, she had saved ten thousand dollars. She used the money to bring thirty-four of her relatives west. She never was able to find her husband and her children who were still in slavery. Shortly before Mrs. Brown's death in 1885, one daughter did make her way to Central City to be reunited with her mother.

Biddy Mason walked from Mississippi to California as a slave, breathing and eating dust behind three hundred wagons. Her job on the trail was to herd the livestock. Once she arrived in California, she challenged her master in one of the most famous trials of the time. The California court set her free because slavery was illegal in that state.

She remained in Los Angeles and became a nurse and housekeeper. Eventually, she invested in real estate and became one of the wealthiest women in California. Always she helped those in need. Her particular interest was to do what she could to promote education for black children. Known as Grandma Mason, she gave to the poor, helped the imprisoned, purchased land for churches, and built schools for nurses.

Mary Fields, also known as Stagecoach Mary, was the first woman the United States Postal Department authorized to carry the mail. Known for her strength and fierce independence, she also had a gentle side that the people of Cascade, Montana, remember. She grew flowers in her garden and attended all of the town's baseball games as an ardent fan.

Introduction: They Don't Tell

Beginning with Kenneth Wiggins Porter's *The Negro on the American Frontier* (New York: Arno, 1971), several historians have recently done much to correct the impression in popular culture that the settling of the West was an all white affair. In 1971 William Loren Katz published *The Black West* (New York: Doubleday, 1971) tracing the role of the black in exploring, taming, and settling the frontier.

Katz begins his book with Stephen Dorantes, or Estevan, the African who explored the Southwest with his Spanish masters, and then led the expedition in which he died. He fought so heroically in his last battle with the Zuni Indians that he became a legendary hero to them even though he was an enemy. Katz moves from the early explorers such as Estevan and York to the fur traders, the Bonga family and Jim Beckwourth, to the early settler to the cowboys, the homesteaders, the Buffalo Soldiers and their dismounted charge up San Juan Hill with Theodore Roosevelt. Katz has also published *The Black Indians: A Hidden Heritage* (New York: Atheneum, 1986) about the runaway blacks who lived with the Indians.

A third historian who has focused on the neglect of the role of blacks in the West is a Missourian, a former Lincoln University professor, William Sherman Savage. His book, *Blacks in the West*, 1976, is a part of the series, *Contributions in Afro-American and African Studies*, published by Greenwood Press. His approach is that of a scholar who carefully documents from published and unpublished sources the role of blacks in "winning the West." He analyzes the black migration and evaluates their economic and occupational positions in the western states. His analysis of the role of blacks in the mining industry is particularly good.

Jack Weston's re-interpretation of the western myth in his book *The American Cowboy* (New York: Shocken Books, 1985) is more narrowly focused than Katz' or Savage's books.

Weston's socialism is quite evident. Still, he has documented very well the role of the minorities, women, Chicanos, and blacks on the frontier:

> *The lily-white popular vision of the conquerors of our West began back long before movies. The scores of commercial photographers of the West who made cheaply reproduced scrapbook souvenir and*

postcard photo prints and graphoscope and stereopticon cards for mass consumption--F. M. Steel, N. H. Rose, C. D. Kirkland, W. J. Carpenter, L. A. Huffman--didn't include blacks in their scenes of cowboy life. The same is true of wood-engraving of photographs or of on-location sketches printed in popular magazines, like Harper's and Leslies' Illustrated Weekly: nary a black cowboy. The all black Ninth and Tenth Cavalry could not be ignored by artists, but black cowboys could and were--Remington painted and sketched many black cavalry soldiers but no black cowboys. The 'Cowboy Fun' part of early Wild West shows had no blacks, nor were they depicted on the lithograph posters and billboards. Our Western myth began to form early on the very frontier it presented and shaped and from the beginning excluded blacks. (153)

In folklore and popular culture this exclusion has continued to the present.

Dozens of other blacks played a role in exploring and settling the West. Their stories largely exist only in the oral history and folklore. Three hundred black laborers laid track on the Union Pacific Railroad working with Irish, Chinese, German, and other immigrants. Emmett J. Scott was one of the first frontier newspaper owners and published The Texas Freeman. W. J. Harding served in the Wyoming legislature. Charles Pettit was appointed Deputy United States Marshall in Kansas. Ed Sanderlin, an early pioneer in Denver, was a barber who became a rich man. The pioneers of both races honored him by attending his funeral. Mifflin Gibbs was a gold prospector, journalist, businessman, and defender of people's rights. When he moved to Arkansas in 1873, he was elected judge and appointed to various government positions by the President of the United States.

The purpose of this book is to bring together the traditions of oral history and folklore through the story-songs of Cecil Williams and the art of Keith Conaway to help rectify the neglect of the black explorers, soldiers, cowboys, pioneers, and settlers in American history and popular culture.

"They Don't Tell"

Songs are made about westerners
And movies about pioneers.
Books they write about gunfighters
And tell of their careers.

Songs are sung about mountain men
who pushed back the frontier.
Of hunters, guides and Indians
And trips of pioneers.

Legends are told in song and story,
But of one race they don't' tell.

(CHORUS)

Where are the tales of the black cowboy
This country knew so well
Where are the tales of the black cowboy
This country knew so well
This country knew so well,

Song and books, fiction and fact,
Are written of early days.
Most forget some cowboys were black
And the truth goes astray.

Legend and truth in song and story,
Has left a great big gap.
To fill this hole just use cowboys,
Whose skins are colored black.

The slaves that Mr. Lincoln freed,
Didn't leave our growing land.
They seemed to vanish in history
Due west 'cross the burning sand.

They Don't Tell

Words and Music:
Cecil Williams

♩= 101

Songs are made a-bout Wes-ter-ners and mo-vies a-bout pio-neers;

books they write a-bout gun figh-ters and tell of their ca-reers;

songs are sung a-bout moun-tain men who pushed back the fron-tier.

Chorus:

Where are the tales of the bla-ck cow-boys the coun-try knew so well?

Where are the tales of the bla-ck cow-boys the coun-try knew so well? coun-try knew so well?

to next verse:

Copyright May 5, 1973 East Palo Alto, CA.

Keith D. Conaway © 2005

Explorers

Estaban

The highest tribute one culture can pay to another is to make a member of an alien culture a part of its folklore and legendry. Estevan became a hero to two cultures alien to his African heritage.

The Zuni Indians, members of the Pueblo tribe, have made Stephen Dorantes, known as Estevan, Estaban, or Little Stephen, such a legend. The Zuni tell of a brave black man who entered their village in what is now Arizona and was slain. As retold by Monroe W. Work in *The Negro Year Book*, 1925, Zuni folklore contains the following:

> *It is to be believed that a long time ago, when roofs lay over the walls of Kyaki-me, then the Black Mexicans came from their abodes in Everlasting Summerland [Mexico]. Then the Indians of Sp-no-li set up a great howl, and thus they and our ancients did much ill to one another. Then and thus was killed by our ancients right where the stone stands down by the arroyo of Kya-ki-me, one of the Black Mexicans, a large man, with chili lips. (Katz 11)*

Estevan also became a hero in Spanish culture because of his role in being among the first leaders of the explorations of the conquistadors in the Southwest. He is the first African to appear in the Spanish historical chronicles of the New World.

However, he was not the first African to come to the New World. According to some historians, Pedro Alonso Nino was a black pilot with Columbus on his first voyage in 1492. There is more evidence to support the claim that Diego el Negro, a cabin boy who accompanied Columbus on his fourth voyage in 1502, was the first black to land in the New World. Naturally, since they were slaves of the Spanish, most of the blacks who came to the New World, during this time, came as laborers, not explorers.

In 1513 thirty blacks were with Balboa when he sailed the first ships on the Pacific coast. Three hundred were with Cortez when he defeated the Aztecs in 1519. They were the laborers who had moved the artillery and did other heavy lifting for his army. One of those black men planted and harvested the first wheat in the New World. Blacks also accompanied Pizarro in his conquest of Peru.

The first black settlers were apparently those who came as slaves with Lucas Vasquez de Ayllon and five hundred Spaniards in 1526. Vasquez established a colony on the Pedee River on what is now the South Carolina coast. The first slave revolt occurred shortly after their arrival. The black settlers turned on their Spanish slave masters and disappeared into the wilderness.

Finding life in the wilderness of the New World more than they could bear without their black servants, the Spanish abandoned their settlement. They returned to Haiti with only one hundred and fifty of the original five hundred settlers surviving.

The fate of the rebellious slaves left by the Spaniards is unknown. Many historians believe they might have survived the hostile wilderness. There is some evidence they commingled their blood with the Indian tribes of the area. Whatever happened to them, as Drotning writes, "the black man clearly has an early priority on the right to call himself an American" (6).

Estevan arrived in the New World two years after this ill-fated first settlement in North America by the Spanish. But he was not just a laborer. Even though he lived and died a slave, he was known as a leader with many skills and heroic virtues among the conquistadors. He became an adviser to Cortez and a guide for Cabeza de Vaca and Father Marcos de Niza. He explored large areas of what became known as Florida, Mexico, Arizona, and New Mexico.

He first came to the New World with his master, Andres Dorantes, in 1528. Dorantes was leading a five-hundred man expedition authorized by King Ferdinand to explore the northern shore of the Gulf of Mexico. Quickly the expedition failed because of storms, other disasters, and incompetent leadership. Disease, desertions, battles, and starvation reduced the party to four, Andres Dorantes, Estevan, and two other whites. The Indians captured

Explorer: Estaban

and enslaved these four. So Estevan was now a slave twice over, first to his Spanish master, and second to the Indians.

Estevan, a strong man physically and a natural leader, led the escape from the Indians. This escape began an eight-year odyssey of the four among the various Indian tribes of the northern Gulf coast. One of the whites who escaped with Estevan recorded that he "was our go-between; he informed himself about the ways we wished to take, what towns there were, and the matters we desired to know" (Katz 7).

Eight years later, the four survivors of the original 500 men in the expedition reached Spanish headquarters in Mexico. There Estevan was rewarded for his heroism and leadership by being sold to Antonio de Mendoza, Viceroy of New Spain.

Estevan's knowledge of the northern Gulf Coast and his stories of the Cibola, or the Seven Cities of Gold, caused Governor Mendoza to decide to send an expedition in search of wealth. Father Marcos de Niza led the explorers with Estevan as the guide. A member of this expedition said about him, "It was the Negro who talked to them [the Indians] all the time; he inquired about the roads we should follow, the villages; in short, about everything we wished to know." (Katz, *Eyewitness*, 7).

Father de Niza sent Estevan ahead with several Indians and two greyhounds. His instructions were to send back wooden crosses of various sizes to indicate how close he was to Cibola. The closer he was to the golden city, the larger the crosses were to be that he returned to Niza.

Just as he and the three whites had done on their earlier journey into the area, Estevan posed as a medicine man. Only on this occasion, he carried a large gourd decorated with strings of bells and a red and white feather. The gourd was thought to be either a source of magic or a symbol of peace to the Indians.

As he marched northward, he sent back to Father de Niza larger and larger crosses indicating he was approaching his goal. Richard Hakluyt in *Hakluyt's Collection of the Early Voyages, Travels, and Discoveries of the English Nation* (London, 1810) quotes Father de Niza as writing,

...within four days after the messengers of Stephan returned unto me with a great cross as high as a man, and they brought me word

The Black West in Story and Song

> *from Stephan, that I should forthwith come away after him, for he had found people which gave him information of a very mighty providence, and that he had sent one of the said Indians. (Katz 11)*

News kept arriving back at the main party that the Indians were giving Estevan vast amounts of leather and turquoise as he progressed. As many as three hundred Indians joined him in his march. This sort of news kept up for weeks. Then there was silence. Before Father de Niza could reach the Zuni town, the Indians had killed Estevan and all the members of his party.

Langston Hughes, perhaps relying on the oral tradition more than other writers, describes his death in the following way.

> *Suspicious of his mission, the Zuni chiefs had ordered their warriors to set upon Estevan and all his band outside the walls of Hawaikuk. And it was there that an arrow pierced him through, and his body cut into pieces as a lesson to other intruders. (20)*

Father de Niza returned to Mexico with stories of the Seven Cities and the bravery of Estevan. Although the Spanish conquistadors never found the seven cities of gold, the search for them and Estevan's bravery encouraged others to continue the search and explore the area. Eventually the Spanish built settlements, missions, military installations, and trading posts there. The land that Estevan first penetrated and explored became an important part of the Spanish Empire in the New World.

"Estaban"

And his eyes were dark as the night,
And his teeth were pearly white.
In one ear lobe he wore Spanish gold.
And his hair was like the robe of a buffalo.

(CHORUS)

Seven years they sailed the seven seas,
Seven cities of gold they sought to find.
The year was 1524, and a stormy night
on the Florida coast.

Three hundred men fought for they lives,
At the rising sun seven survived.
Six Conquistadors and one more,
A black an African a Moor.

Seven years they fought that burning
sand, From the Florida coast to
the Rio Grand.
Mexico they made their way, Estaban
led the way.

North to Zuni land, Estaban led
another band.
A Zuni arrow dug into his side,
An African brother died.

Until this day the mystery still remain,
And those treasures of Cibola are
yet unclaimed!

(CHORUS)

Estaban! Estaban!

Estaban

Words and Music:
Cecil Williams

♩= 87

And his eyes were as - dark as the night,

and his teeth - were pearl - y white -.

In one ear - - lobe he wore Span - ish gold -,

and his hair was like the robe of the Buf - fa - lo.

Chorus:

Es - ta - ban, Es -ta - ban.

to next verse:

Copyright   East Palo Alto, CA.

A Map of
LEWIS & CLARK'S TRACK

York

Much of the romance of the Lewis and Clark expedition is focused on the Shoshone woman, Sacajawea, or Bird Woman, who acted as the guide and interpreter for the Corps of Discovery. She was the only woman to accompany the great explorers. But York, the slave and life-long companion of William Clark, also played a major role in the expedition's success.

Most of the Indian tribes that Lewis and Clark encountered had never seen a "black, white man," as they called York. Clark used the curiosity of the Indians to good advantage. When the explorers stopped at the Arikara villages, York was tremendously popular with them. He told the Indians that he was a wild animal whom his master had caught and tamed. To make the Indians believe his tall tale he showed his physical strength.

He was over six feet tall and weighed more than 200 pounds. He was able to do feats of lifting and jumping that amazed the Indians. To enforce the idea that he was once a wild animal, he roared, sending the Indian children running away in fear. Clark worried that York "had made himself more tribal than we wished him to do" (Ferris, *National Park Service*, 107).

Whatever the case, York proved invaluable in many other ways on expedition. He was an excellent fisherman, hunter, trapper, and riverman. He was quick to pick up enough of the Indians' language to aid Sacajawea and Charboneau in translating. He learned to read the trail signs and act as a guide. He, Francis Labuiche, and Charboneau were also the only members of the expedition who spoke French. The Indians that the Lewis and Clark expedition encountered had some knowledge of French from trading with fur-trappers, making York's, LaBuiche's, and Charboneau's linguistic abilities invaluable.

His sense of humor in dealing with the Indians' fascination with his blackness enabled other members of the expedition to understand the Indians.

The Black West in Story and Song

At Fort Mandan, the Minitari principal chief Le Borgne (One-Eye) thought that his color was some kind of trick. Le Borgne, with moistened fingers, tried to rub the black off York's skin. The chief had assumed Clark's servant was a white man painted black. He was astonished when he could not change the color of York's skin. Only when he examined the dark skin of York's scalp could he accept that he was a black man.

Later, in Shoshone country, Lewis arrived at the planned rendezvous well ahead of Clark. He had persuaded the Shoshones to wait even though they feared the Blackfeet would attack. Lewis told them that when Clark arrived he would show them a man, "who was black and had short curling hair" (Ambrose 276). Their fear of an attack from the Blackfeet was overcome by their curiosity in seeing a "black white man."

The fact that York continues to exist as a curiosity and legend in Indian folklore is illustrated by the tale the Flatheads tell about him.

> *One of the strange men was black. He had painted himself in charcoal, my people thought. In those days it was the custom for warriors, when returning from battle to prepare themselves before reaching camp. Those who had been brave and fearless, the victorious ones in battle, painted themselves in charcoal. So the black man, they thought, had been the bravest of his party (Katz 15).*

Obviously, the Indian lore is wrong about the reason for York's blackness. The lore is right in that York was, if not the bravest, among the bravest of the thirty-three in the Corps of Discovery.

By 1895 both he and Sacajewea were so invaluable Lewis and Clark gave them equal voice with the other members of the Corps. They asked them to vote on such matters as the location of the winter camp. Sixty years before the 15th Amendment gave blacks the right to vote, York, as a member of the Corps of Discovery, became the first black man to vote on American soil. Sacajewea, more than one hundred years before the 19th Amendment gave women the right to vote, became the first woman and first Native America to vote.

When the Corps of Discovery returned to St. Louis in 1806, the people of the city greeted them as heroes. Even York was treated as a hero. Clark allowed

Explorer: York

him to mingle with the crowds and tell stories about their epic journey for several days after their return. York became well known in the taverns of St. Louis as a gifted story-teller. Soon Clark required him to resume his role as his personal servant. York repeatedly asked Clark for his freedom, but Clark did not grant it. In his report to the War Department, the official roster of the Corps did not include York's name.

Clark later did give York a wagon and six-horse team, which he used for hauling freight from Nashville to Richmond.

Perhaps because he longed for the mountains, his freight business failed. More likely, a black man trying to compete for freight business with white teamsters did not have much of a chance. He went from one odd job to another after that.

Again Indian lore enters into the story of York. Some tribes tell of a huge black man who married an Indian woman and became their chief. Such would have been a fitting end for York. However, the historical records indicate that he did not find his freedom in the mountains he had explored and grown to love.

He died on an unknown date, sometime after 1816, somewhere in Tennessee. According to Clark family lore, his loyalty to his master remained steadfast to the end. He was apparently on his way back to St. Louis to visit Clark when he became ill with cholera and died.

Today it is difficult for us to understand why Clark kept York enslaved after 1806. Part of the answer is in the paternal attitude of Clark and other slave owners. If Clark freed York, what would happen to him? He might be captured illegally by slave catchers or "patty-rollers" [patrollers] and illegally sold "Down South" into harsher slavery. He might not be able to make a living if granted freedom. This was the dilemma slave owners faced. As Jefferson said, it was like having a wolf by the ears.

Still Clark's paternalism was self-serving. York was a valuable piece of property, who often caused him problems. York asked to be allowed to move Louisville to be near his wife. Clark would only let him to go for a visit. Allowing him to go for a visit shows how much trust Clark had that York would not run away. That trust was shown earlier when one of Clark's other slaves ran away.

Lewis gave York four dollars to search for the man, and York brought him back.

Clark was troubled by owning slaves. He wrote his brother, Jonathan that he felt "much vexed & perplexed by my few negrows [sic]." He considered selling them not only because of the frustration they caused but because he needed money. Still, he felt some guilt about selling them and yet could not, with his paternalistic and racial attitudes, set them free.

In May, 1809, York returned to St. Louis to resume his duties as Clark's personal servant. Clark wrote his brother, "York brought my horse. He is here but of little Service [sic] to me, insolent and sulky. I gave him a Severe [sic] trouncing." (Ambrose 457-58)

Such attitudes expressed by Clark and other slave owners are beyond our comprehension today. To "trounce" a man who had been a close companion all of his life, who had been a leader on their expedition, and to show so little concern for York's personal life are traits that even enlightened slave owners such as Clark held. Today, we cannot forgive them or even understand them. As Jefferson wrote about slave owners, "The man must be a prodigy who can retain his manners and his morals undepraved [sic] by such circumstances." (Cooke 189)

Apparently by 1811, Clark decided to give York his freedom. In an interview with Washington Irving, Clark quoted York as saying, "Damn this freedom. I have never had a happy day since I got it."

Still Clark was enlightened enough to free several of his slaves, knowing that they would face harsh laws and dangers and prejudiced white people who would want them re-enslaved.

"York"

When America was young and a'struggling to be free,
She found herself surrounded by the big three.
To the North was the Union Jack, and South West was mighty Spain,
The Atlantic to the east but the French owned New Orleans.

Our history books have told us of a purchase that was made.
And the sum of fifteen million to the French
for land was paid.

(CHORUS)

There was Lewis, There was Clark.
Sacajewa, There was York. He was free to
die but not be free!

On a rainy day in May, And the year was 1804
just a brave little party numbering only twenty-four.
From the mighty Mississippi to the golden Pacific shore,
Up the wide, wide Missouri heading west to explore.
From St. Louie to St. Charles, Fort Mandan
to Yellowstone. Three hard years on the
trail, Exploring the great wild unknown.

(CHORUS)

Past the Great Falls they did struggle and
Three Rivers running wild, Through the
Lemiah and the Lost Trail Pass they crossed
The Continental Divide.
On the Lolo Trail they lost their way, half-starved they nearly died.
And on horse meat and candle wax they managed to survive.

Well those Captains earned their medals and
with glory there came fame, Soldier men
earned fortune and for pay, land they claimed.
York earned his freedom eleven years from that
day, He never go a nickel or a penny for his pay.
But he returned up stream again, to marry an Indian
Maiden and be his own man.
These were the Heroes of the hour! Brave souls of yesteryear,
They helped to make our country, The one we love so dear!

York

Words and Music by:
Cecil Williams

When America was young and a strugglin' to be free, She found herself surrounded then by the big three. To the North was the Union Jack and Southwest was mighty Spain, The Atlantic to the East but the French owned New Orleans. Now our his't'ry books have told us that a purchase was once made, and a sum of fifteen million to the French for land was paid. On a rainy day in May, and the year was eighteen o-four, Just a brave lil' party num-b'rin' only twenty four. From the mighty Mississippi to the golden Pacific shore, Up the wide, wide Missouri heading west to explore-. From St. Louie to St. Charles Fort Mandan to Yellow Stone, Three hard years upon the trail explorin' the great wild unknown.

Chorus:
There was Lewis, there was Clark, Sacajawea, there was York. He was free to die but not to be free.

to next verse:

Copyright 1977 East Palo Alto, CA.

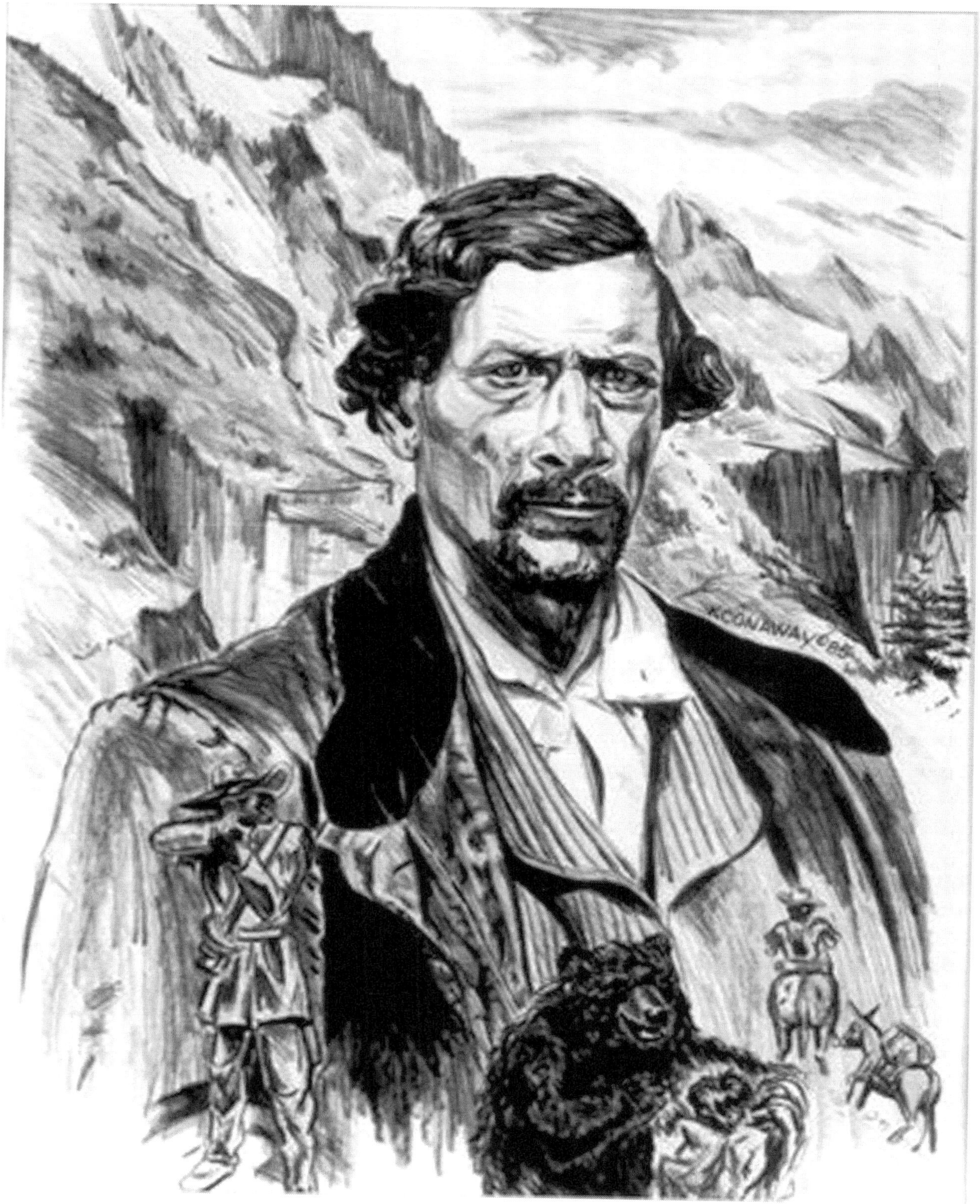
KCONAWAY©85

James Beckwourth

James Beckwourth, the most adventurous of the mountain men, was never lost when he fur-trapped or lived as a chief of the Crow nation in the Absaroka. But he became lost in American history behind the names of Hugh Glass, Jim Bridger, Jedediah Smith, Kit Carson, and other great mountain men.

Francis Parkman wrote in his copy on the flyleaf of Beckwourth's autobiography, "Much of the narrative is probably false. Beckwith [a variant spelling of his name] is a fellow of bad character--a compound of black and white blood" (Bontemps, p.30). Other historians considered Beckwourth to be a liar because his adventures seemed to be more than any one man could have possibly experienced.

Harrison Clifford Dale, unconcerned with the mixture of Beckwourth's blood, set out in 1918 to check the veracity of his experiences and found most of them to be authentic. Certainly in exaggerating his experiences, Beckwourth was following the tall-tale tradition of the American frontier from Boone and Crockett through Bowie and Earp down to the present. But even a careful researcher such as Bernard De Voto found it difficult to accept Beckwourth's claims.

De Voto's analysis of his autobiography in *Across the Wide Missouri* illustrates this skepticism:

> [*The Life and Adventures of James P. Beckwourth*] is one of the gaudiest books in our literature and may well be the goriest: at least more Indians are killed in it than in any other book known to this student. Various writers have appraised it variously but, apart from yarns in which Jim unnecessarily quadruples his own daring,

> *it is in the main trustworthy and is sometimes an indispensable witness to the events it deals with (128).*

Despite calling it "in the main trustworthy" and "sometimes indispensable," De Voto gives the rest of his analysis over to proving Beckwourth's version of his feud with Tom Fitzpatrick to be untrue. De Voto did conclude in *Life and Adventures* that the autobiography is a personal story and should be read as mythology rather than as truth or falsehood.

Still Beckwourth has not become a part of American mythology as Bridger, Carson, Glass, and Smith have. Certainly his adventures and tall tales put him in that company. Apparently his race has kept him out of American history and folklore. Beckwourth himself must have recognized his race as a barrier because he makes no mention of it in the autobiography and takes pains to give emphasis to his roots in Virginia.

Beckwourth's father was a Virginian and a veteran of the Revolutionary War who immigrated to a settlement at the confluence of the Mississippi and Missouri Rivers. That village became known as the Beckwourth Settlement, about twelve miles down river from St. Charles. Jim's mother was one of Beckwourth's slaves. Jim was apprenticed to the blacksmith George Casner of St. Louis in 1812. From adolescence onward he had a strong will, great pride, and interest in women. His courtship of a lady and the late hours he kept caused him to have first, an argument with Casner, then a fight, and finally, a legal dispute when Jim was 19.

Jim fled to Illinois where he developed his skills as a hunter of game for miners at Galena. After accumulating seven hundred dollars from his hunting, he then went to New Orleans. There yellow fever and the closed society of the South made him decide that the frontier was the place where he could find freedom.

He joined General William Henry Ashley's Rocky Mountain Fur Company and soon became an expert horseman, trapper, Indian fighter, and scout. By Ashley's own account, Jim rescued him from drowning in the Green River. Ashley valued his skills as a mountain man so much that shortly after their return to St. Louis he paid him $1000 to deliver a message to William L. Sublette, the leader of the trappers in the Great Salt Lake area. Upon delivering

Explorer: James Beckwourth

Ashley's message, Jim accepted from Sublette the mission to establish an outpost with the Blackfeet.

He succeeded in his mission with the Blackfeet so well that the tribe gave him two wives. When he left the Blackfeet, he honored his two wives by giving them dress patterns from Sublette's trading post.

Beckwourth's greatest Indian involvement was with the Crows, who considered him to be a long lost member of the tribe kidnapped by the Cheyenne. With his acceptance into the Crow nation he acquired a mother, father, brothers, sisters, and a new wife, Still Water.

He threw himself whole-heartedly into the life of the Crows. Quickly he became a leading warrior who was honored with such names as Bull's Robe and Medicine Calf. Finally, with the death of Rotten Belly, the Crows made him a chief of the tribe.

Apparently civilization still had a hold upon him. After fourteen years in the mountains, he returned to St. Louis. There he found that his fiancé, whom he had left nearly a decade and a half earlier to go on a mission for Ashley into the Salt Lake region, had married just two weeks before his return. He then returned to the Crows, and married Fallen Leaf, or in some accounts, Pine Leaf. She was a woman warrior who had made the vow not to marry until she had taken 100 scalps to avenge her brother's death.

Still he felt restlessness. Five weeks after their marriage he left the Crows to wander from St. Louis to New Orleans to Florida to Mexico to California. In California, he fought Indians as a scout for the United States army. Later he guided wagons across the Rockies, discovered a pass that is named after him, acquired a Mexican wife, and operated a ranch on the Feather River.

In California he met T. D. Bonner to whom he dictated his autobiography which was published by Harper and Brothers in 1856. Also in California he was accused of being involved in horse rustling and discreetly left for Denver where he operated a store for Sublette and married still again.

Finally, in the twilight of his life he was asked by the United States to return to the Crow nation in an attempt to pacify them. At Absaroka he was greeted by great warmth by his old Indian companions. Authorities disagree about his death at this time. Some accept the Crow legend that at a tribal feast Beckwourth refused to lead the tribe again. Because he rejected the proposal of being chief again, the Crows poisoned him, concluding that if they could not have him as a live chief, they would at least keep him with them always in the tribal burial ground. Katz believes that Beckwourth died of food poisoning on his way to the Crow nation, while Bontemps, Conroy, and others believe he died accidentally of food poisoning while feasting with the Crows.

Whatever the circumstances of his death, he is a mythic figure in the American West. In the Rocky Mountains, he found freedom from slavery and humiliation. He ranged restlessly among the Indians, Mexicans, and whites as a figure larger than life who was a hunter, trapper, horseman, warrior, and trailblazer representing the best and worst of American frontiersman.

"Jim Beckwourth Black Mountain Man"

Jim left St. Louie in the spring of twenty-four,
Spring of twenty-four, year Eighteen Twenty-Four.

Two friends with him they rode, The Lord up above
and his trust Forty-Four, That 'ol Hawkins Forty-Four.

Strangers he trusted none, and no man's allegiance
did he pledge, Be you Red, Black or White you
treat me right, I'll do the same.

(CHORUS)

Jim Beckwourth was a Black Mountain Man,
A hunter, trapper and a famous guide.
He explored both mountain and desert sand,
And was a Chief of the Crow Tribe.

Jim rode courier for the U.S. Calvary during
the war with The Seminoles, And in 1847 he
fought with General Kearney during the war
with Mexico!

Medicine Calf he was called by the council of
Crow, and during his legendary fame Iron Claw
he was named by the Cheyenne and the Arapaho.

(CHORUS)

In a cabin in the Sierra Mountains, Jim Beckwourth
settled down, Where he lived until it
was time to return to his happy hunting ground.
Now in California there still remain signs of
his great fame
A town, a mountain, and a pass still bear that
Beckwourth name.

Black Mountain Man
Jim Beckworth

Words and music by:
Cecil Williams
& Ray Garrett

Jim left St. Louis in the spring of twenty four --. Two friends with him they rode --. The good Lord up above and his trusty forty four, the Lord up above, and his hawkin' forty four --, that ol' hawkin' forty four --. Strangers he trusted none, no man's allegiance did he pledge -, be he red, black or white -, You treat me right, I'll do the same --

Chorus:
Jim Beckworth was a Black Mountain Man -. A hunter, a trapper, and a famous guide -. He explored both mountains and desert sand He was a chief of the Crow tribe -.

Copyright March 14, 1973 East Palo Alto, CA.

to next verse:

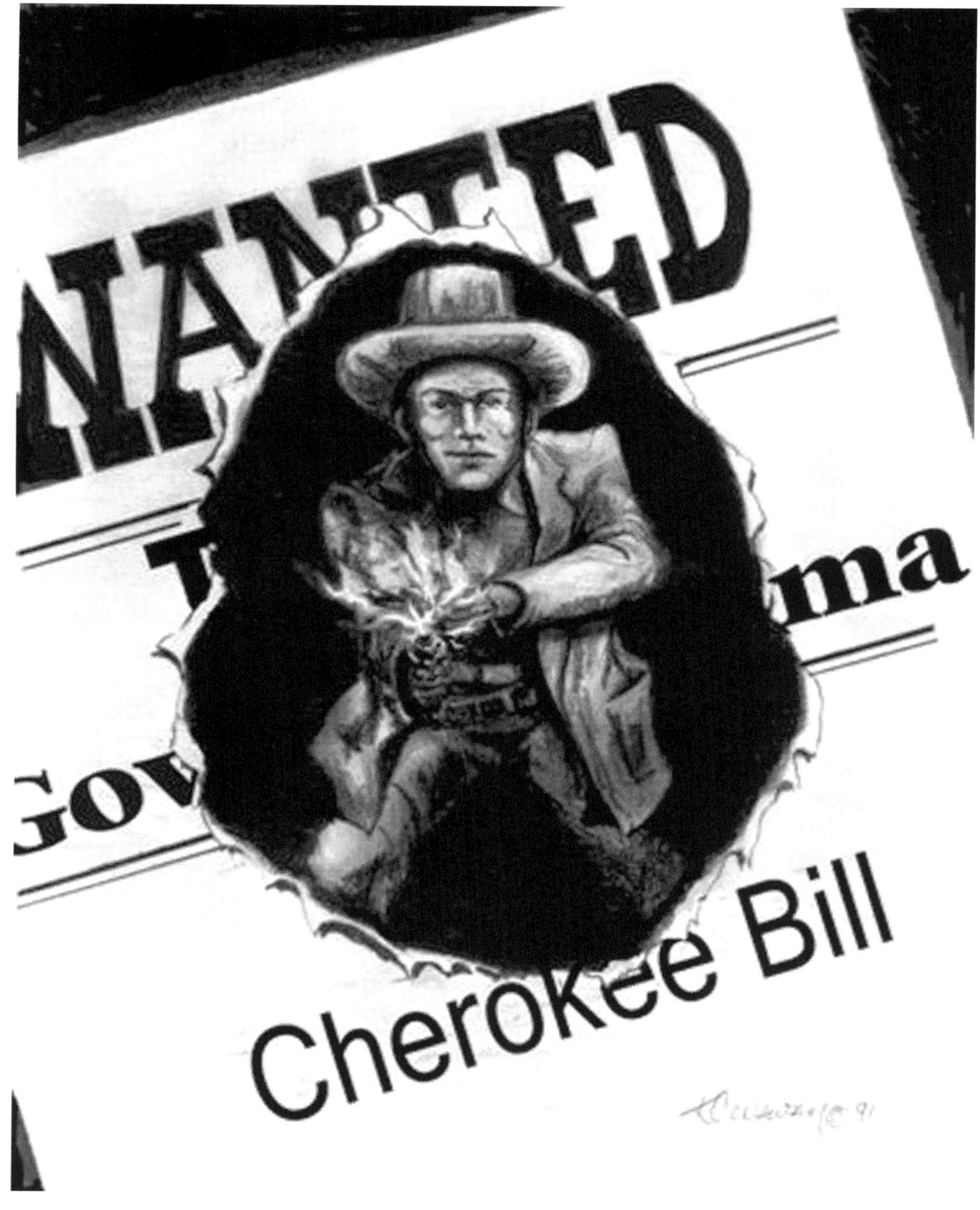
Cherokee Bill

Outlaws and Lawmen

Cherokee Bill

To Judge Isaac Parker, the hanging judge of Fort Smith, Arkansas, and probably to the large, predominantly white crowd who witnessed his execution, Cherokee Bill was a criminal. As Parker said when he pronounced the death sentence, "...human monster from whom innocent people can expect no safety." Judge Parker also told him, "You are undoubtedly the most ferocious monster, and your record more atrocious than all the criminals who have hitherto stood before this bar" (Katz 154-55).

But for many blacks and Indians on the frontier, Cherokee Bill was a heroic figure gone wrong. To them he followed too closely his mother's advice, "Stand up for your rights; don't let anyone impose on you" (Katz 153). During his trial, his friend and fellow outlaw, Bill Cook boasted, "No bars can hold Cherokee" (*Black Indians* 160).

Cook's boast nearly came true, when after his trial ended someone, possibly his mother, smuggled a gun into his cell in the basement of the Fort Smith Federal Courthouse and Jail. He almost escaped, killing one deputy and wounding another before he was recaptured. Judge Parker then delivered his famous statement about his ferocity and expressed regret he had no worse penalty than execution for him.

Nevertheless, just as many white outlaws in the Oklahoma territory such as Bill Doolin and the Dalton brothers were heroes to the white underclass, Cherokee Bill was a hero to many blacks and Indians. His outlaw career was quite similar to Billy the Kid's. Both died in early manhood, but Cherokee Bill had what William Bonney lacked in looks, charm, and height. He was over six feet tall and had a joy of life that caused many who knew him, Indians, blacks, and white, to remember him "...as full of life and the joy of living as ever passed this way" (*Black Indians* 160).

Unlike Billy the Kid who was far from handsome, Cherokee Bill was a handsome, copper-skinned man who wore his wavy black hair at shoulder length. He was always well dressed in expensive clothes and a Stetson. His bridle was silver and his rope was black and white horse hair.

He was born Crawford Goldsby on the right side of the law in Fort Concho, Texas. His father, George Goldsby, was a sergeant in the U. S. Tenth Cavalry Regiment, the most famous of the Buffalo Soldier units in the West. Tension between the Buffalo Soldiers and the white Texans existed throughout his early years. Only two years after he was born, his father deserted to avoid trial on an accusation of shooting at white homesteaders. Such shooting incidents were common between the soldiers and whites at this time.

His mother, forced to move frequently to find employment, often left Bill and his younger brother alone. She did enroll him in school in Cherokee, Kansas, for three years. Then she sent him to the Carlisle Indian School in Pennsylvania for two years.

Returning from the East, he began to engage in the life of freedom on the Cherokee reservation. By 1894, he was eighteen and had not been involved in any serious trouble. For awhile he visited the Red Fork Ranch. There he was known for the entertaining stories about himself he was constantly telling. In the evening he sang songs, danced jigs, and good naturedly talked to everyone.

His dark, handsome looks and his devil may care personality made him quite attractive to women. This apparently led to a fight at a dance with a black man named Jake Lewis. Lewis beat him in a fair fistfight, according to eyewitnesses. Two days later Bill killed him in a gunfight. Fleeing into the hills, he joined the Cook gang, where he killed a member of a posse that had surrounded their hideout.

Apparently this killing made Bill realize that his days were numbered. He went on a killing and robbery spree throughout the territory, murdering a barber during a bank holdup, a station agent and a conductor in separate train robberies, and Ernest Melton, a bystander in a post office robbery in Lenapah. Because Melton was unarmed and a prominent citizen of Lenapah, Cherokee Bill then became the most wanted man in the territory.

Legends began to grow about his daring escapes and his speed with a Colt revolver. These tales caused lawmen to pursue him at a safe distance. Bill said

Outlaws and Lawmen: Cherokee Bill

shortly before his death that his speedy gunfire was not always accurate, but it rattled his opponent enough to prevent him from being hit. Other legends indicate that he was on such good terms with the Indians of the territory that he could travel through their lands while the posse pursuing him could not.

His legendary prowess with women also aided him in his two years of flight. Tales tell of many women, who finding him irresistibly attractive, hid him from the lawmen.

One such woman, Effie Crittendon, tried to aid him and the Cook brothers in collecting the $265.70 federal money for their share in confiscated Cherokee land. She took their money orders to Tahlequah, collected the money, but was followed back to their hiding place. In the gunfight that followed, Cherokee Bill and Bill Cook escaped, but Jim Cook was wounded and captured.

Soon though another woman, Maggie Glass, caused him to be captured. She was a black Cherokee woman who went with him to her cousin's home for dinner one evening, failing to tell him that her cousin was Ike Rogers, a U. S. deputy marshal. The marshal tried to arrest and in the hand-to-hand struggle that followed Bill was knocked unconscious by a piece of firewood. Some say that Maggie hit Bill from behind with the firewood as he struggled with the deputy marshal.

He was handcuffed and placed in Roger's wagon. On the way to jail he broke his cuffs. Rogers, armed with a Winchester, quickly stopped his escape. A large posse of black and white marshals then transported him to Fort Smith, Arkansas, in chains.

There he posed for pictures with the deputies, where he was obviously the center of attention in a large crowd. His demeanor in the photograph is casual, relaxed, and nonchalant. He is taller than all the others in the picture. He reflects an air of confidence while the others are wooden and staring, in awe of the camera or Bill or both.

His trial before Judge Parker was swift as were most of the hanging judge's trials. A large crowd had gathered for the court term that year, but the largest crowd ever had come to town when they heard that Cherokee Bill was on trial. He was convicted of the murder of the unarmed bystander killed in the Lenapah post office holdup. Before he was sentenced, he was being held in a basement cell at the Fort Smith Federal Courthouse. Both of his lawyer's appeals to the Supreme Court were rejected. Judge Parker sentenced him to die on March 17, 1896.

An even larger crowd than usual gathered for the hanging at six that morning. The Fort Smith newspaper reported that Bill approached the gallows "singing and whistling." The area around the gallows was filled to capacity with over one hundred spectators as he walked the last mile with his mother at his side. He remained calm, and looking at the crowd he joked, "Looks like something is going to happen."

He then climbed the scaffold. When the marshal in charge asked him if he had any last words, he said quite calmly, "No, I came here to die--not make a speech." At twenty years of age he was executed.

In a two-year time span from age eighteen to twenty, he had killed at least twelve men and wounded many others. His fearless bravado in gunfights and his apparent courage in facing death by hanging, made him a legend among the Indians, blacks, and even whites in Oklahoma. Many feel his exploits should have made him as famous an outlaw as Jesse James and Billy the Kid. But he was black and is now almost forgotten except for the court records of Judge Parker, a few newspaper stories, and most of all, the tales blacks and Indians still tell. Was he a hero? Only in the sense that Jesse James and Billy the Kid are.

"Cherokee Bill"

I'll sing you a ballad about Cherokee Bill,
A young desperado of those Oklahoma hills.
This story is true and now must be told,
This is how it happened, many, many years ago.

(CHORUS)

Cherokee - , Cherokee -
This is the legend of Cherokee Bill

Bill's dad was a soldier of the tenth calvary,
His mother was a maiden of the tribe of Cherokee.
He was gracious, he was handsome and as charming as could be,
A lover of ladies throughout the territory.

He was a man among men, many Indians were his friends
Many times he did ride with the five civilized tribes
Cherokee, Choctaw, Chickasaw, Seminole, and Creek
Cherokee, Choctaw, Chickasaw, Seminole, and Creek

Riding, shooting, fighting, he was wild, he was free,
He was a cold-blooded killer, so says our history.
Bill made legend in the wild and wooly West,
Outriding posses and outshooting the best.

Around his waist he wore pearl-handled .44's
His draw was lightning fast, second best, you'd breathed your last.
He robbed stagecoaches, banks, and trains, adding to his infamous fame.
Twenty notches or more were carved on his .44's.

He was vicious as a rattler, he was bronze tan, and lean,
This natural born killer was only nineteen.
One dark night where Bill stayed, he was tricked and betrayed.
Handcuffed and shackle-bound, then taken into town.

Word soon spread throughout the land, they finally caught that killerman.
News spread far and wide, Bill's been caught, now he'll be tried.
From St. Louie people came, all aboard a special train,
Chicago, Dallas too, Abilene and Sioux City Sioux.

The ol' hanging judge asked this day, "Bill! Have you a word to say?"
Bill just stood there straight and tall, making not a sound at all

Cherokee Bill

Words and Music by:
Cecil Williams

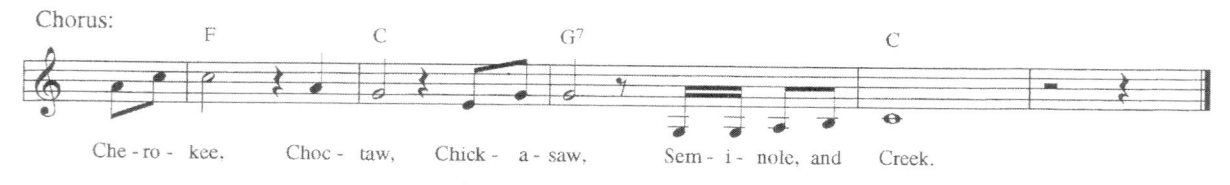

I'll sing you a bal-lad a-bout Cher-o-kee Bill. Young des-per-a-do of those O-kla-ho-ma hills. The sto-ry is true so - now it can be told. This is how it hap-pened many years a-go. Bills dad was a sol-dier of the tenth ca-val-ry, His mo-ther was a mai-den of the tribe of Cher-o-kee. He was gra-cious, he was hand-some and as charm-ing as could be, A lo-ver of the la-dies thru out the ter-ri-to-ry He was a man a-mong men, Man-y in-dians were his friends, Man-y times did he ride, With the five ci-vi-lized tribes.

Chorus:
Che-ro-kee, Choc-taw, Chick-a-saw, Sem-i-nole, and Creek.

Copyright May 28, 1975 East Palo Alto, CA.

to next verse:

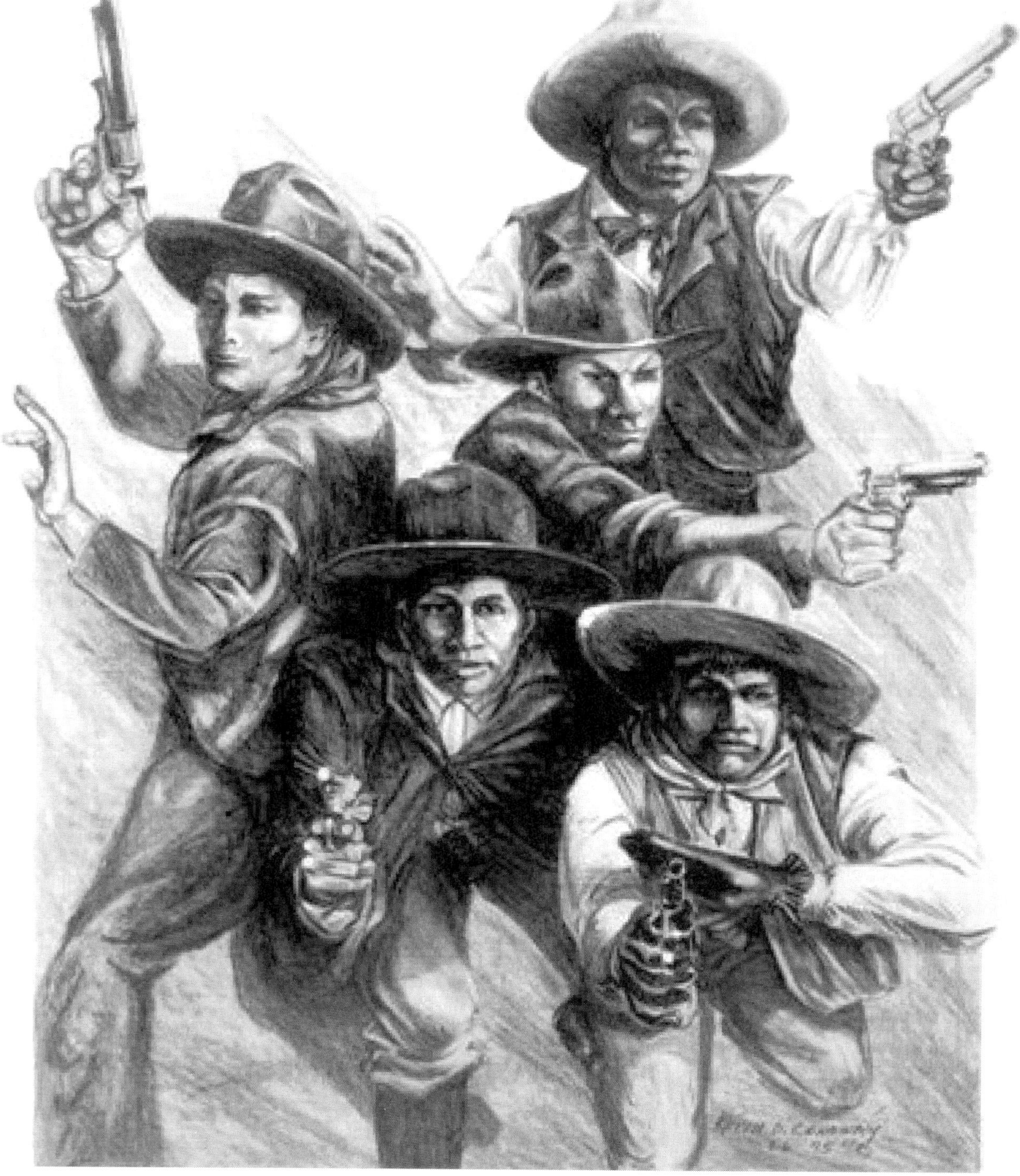

The Rufus Buck Gang

The Rufus Buck Gang could not articulate their resentments, so they went on one of the deadliest crime sprees in American history. By the time they had finished, they had committed murder, rape, robbery, and mayhem throughout the Oklahoma Territory. Yet the members of this vicious gang, Rufus Buck, Sam Sampson, Maoma July, and Lewis and Luckey [sic] Davis were just five adolescents.

What caused their crimes? Perhaps it was just they were born bad, as many in the Territory said; or perhaps the years of discrimination and racism had reached its height in them. When they raped Mrs. Rosetta Hassan, Rufus Buck declared he was Cherokee Bill's brother, implying they were emulating Bill and other outlaws. Or perhaps, it was the resentment of seeing the government take their tribal lands and the hatred they felt toward those who hated them. They were outcasts in white society because they were black. They were outcasts in the Indian society for the same reason.

They probably knew they were doomed when they killed one of Judge Isaac Parker's U. S. marshals. John Garrett, a black Indian, was keeping too close an eye on them outside of Okmulgee. Whatever the motivation for their crimes was, they could not themselves explain it.

They did not testify at their own trial before Judge Parker. On the gallows they made no last statements. Only Lucky Davis said anything as they waited to die. He saw his sister in the crowd and shouted to her, "Good-bye, Martha." With that, the five members of the gang were simultaneously hanged from Parker's famous multiple scaffold.

The photograph taken of them the day before their execution shows them handcuffed together. Katz vividly describes their appearance. "Except for the handcuffs holding them together, they might be mistaken for a junior high school athletic team. There is no demented look, no savage ferocity on their faces, just young men, hanging out somewhere" (Black Indians 164). Anyone looking at the picture would be struck by their youthfulness and probably wonder how they could have engaged in such a series of brutal crimes.

The Black West in Story and Song

In Oklahoma oral tradition there is some talk of their engaging in their crimes for political reasons or to drive all the whites out of Oklahoma. There is neither documentary nor eyewitness evidence to support this. Their criminal career lasted only thirteen days, beginning July 28, and ending August 10, 1895. Eleven months later, on July 1, 1896, they were hanged. They would have had little time to express their motives even if they had been articulate enough or literate enough to do so. Now all we can do is look at the old photograph and wonder.

Katz wonders too if the motive for their crimes was political when he couples their activities with the ruling of the United States Supreme Court in Plessey vs. Ferguson. That decision made separate but equal facilities the law of the land in the same year they were hanged. "The appearance at the same moment in history of the most violent Black Indian outbreaks [Cherokee Bill's and the Rufus Buck Gang crimes] in the U. S. and the high court's decision may not be totally accidental" (Black Indians 165). Katz's tone in presenting this as a possibility reveals that he does not accept the political explanation for their violence.

Yet we know that for succeeding generations they became symbols of the brutalization that blacks in the territory experienced. Many today argue that their brutality was caused by the hatred and cruelty they had experienced themselves. Still they were an aberration. They were five adolescents, who for reasons still not understood, killed more people than the Belle Starr and the Dalton gangs combined.

Judge Parker was not a racist in sentencing them to die. As the hanging judge he had sentenced whites, blacks, and Indians to death without prejudice. He had a reputation as a United States Congressman as being the friend of the Indians. When he appointed his two hundred United States deputy marshals to bring law and order to the territory, he seems to have done so without concern for race. He appointed blacks and Indians as well as whites.

The Rufus Buck Gang was also without prejudice in their crimes. The first man they killed was a black marshal appointed by Judge Parker, John Garrett. So the motive for their crimes cannot be called political or racial. Perhaps their crimes were the only way they could articulate the despair and desperation of their lives.

"Rufus Buck Gang"

We know the legend of Robin Hood and the bandits of Sherwood Forest,
The famous name of Jessie James and the plight of Pretty Boy Floyd.
But there were gangs of a different hue, I'll share a few with you,
Their cause and deeds were just as noble, but another point of view.

(CHORUS)

Law and order we've heard the cry, "justice for all", we preach.
Now friends I'm asking, do we always practice what we preach?

Now the records say of their day, The G-men stole their land.
And then one day gave it away, with the run of '89.
So the FBIs were left high and dry, as were their next of kin,
Land all gone and the law of the land was far from being a friend.

(CHORUS)

Well Rufus Buck and ol' Dick Glass understood their plight,
Since they were the next of kin they tried to set things right.
Now the law of the land didn't seem to care about their demand,
Then six-shooter justice is the only law man sometimes understands.
Law and order was cast aside, there was no common ground,
Good men, bad men, black and white gunned each other down.

(CHORUS)

Law and order we've heard the cry, "justice for all", we preach.
Now friends I'm asking, do we always practice what we preach?

Rufus Buck Gang

Words and Music by:
Cecil Williams

We know the legend of Robin Hood and the bandits of Sherwood forest, the famous name of Jesse James and the plight of Pretty Boy Floyd. But there were gangs of a diff'rent hue I'll share a few with you, the cause and deeds were just as noble but another point of view. Law and order, we've heard the cry, justice for all we preach. Now friends I'm as-kin' do we always practice what we preach!

Copyright July 25, 1988   Rolla, MO.

Keith D. Conaway © 2003

Bass Reaves

Judge Parker's lack of racial prejudice served him well in enforcement of the law, particularly in his appointment of marshals. These men, black, white, and red worked for $500 or less a year, and faced danger and death as they policed seventy-four thousand square miles of the Oklahoma Territory. They could earn extra money from bounties. To collect these bounties, they usually had to go into hostile territory and towns where citizens protected the outlaws out of fear, admiration, kinship, or the hope of immunity from terrorism.

Among the 200 marshals Parker appointed were Neely Factor, Bob L. Fortune, John Garrett (killed by the Rufus Buck Gang), Bill Colbert, John Joss, Eugene Walker, Dick Roebuck, Ike Rogers (who captured Cherokee Bill), Morgan Tucker, Grant Johnson, Robert Love, and Bass Reaves. All of these men were black. To their credit, they usually brought back their man alive for trial at Fort Smith when frontier law very often did not concern itself with such niceties. Wanted dead or alive, usually meant dead.

By all accounts, both historical and folkloric, the greatest of these marshals was Bass or Baz Reaves who served Isaac Parker the entire twenty-one years of his tenure as federal judge at Fort Smith. Parker, Reaves, and the other marshals brought law and order to Oklahoma and helped change that territory from an asylum for outlaws to the state by 1907. Although Parker's justice was often brutal and barbaric, it was administered equally to all races at a time when the courts seldom upheld the rights of Indians and blacks. Certainly minority rights were of little concern to most of the white settlers struggling for survival on homesteads and small ranches.

Reaves followed the standard of justice set by Parker, which was to bring outlaws back alive whenever possible. Whenever bringing them back alive was impossible, Parker ordered his deputies to kill to stop them from committing further mayhem and murder. Bass admitted killing fourteen outlaws, but he claimed he never drew his gun first. In allowing his opponents that advantage, he risked death often. He had his horse's reins shot in two, a button shot from his shirt, his hat shot off, and his belt cut by bullets.

Yet most of his arrests did not involve shooting. He used disguises and his powers of observation and deduction much as a modern detective does to catch those wanted dead or alive. In Reaves' thirty-seven years as a law enforcement officer only one man he had a warrant for escaped. Hellubee Smith was too elusive to bring to Judge Parker's court.

In a time of desperate men who would do whatever was necessary to escape the law and in a time when resisting arrest only caused a year to be added to the criminal's sentence, Reaves was never wounded. His native intelligence, his ability to speak Indian languages, his understanding of the cultures of the three races and his adaptability to an untamed environment made him one of the most successful of the western lawmen. Today we remember Wyatt Earp, Bat Masterson, and Wild Bill Hickok in popular culture. Few know the name Bass Reaves.

"Baz Reeves"

It was in July and the year was '75,
Two hundred U.S. Marshals were deputized.
"Law and order," he cried. "We'll turn this thing around,"
That ol' hangin' judge had come to town,
One of most famous of that breed,
Was a black lawman named Baz Reeves.

(CHORUS)

He was a lawman' lawman,
A legend of his time.
Thirty-seven long years,
He laid his life on the line.

Horses shot from under him, bullet holes through his hat brim.
Buttons shot from his shirt, gunbelt shot in two.
In God he placed his faith, but his .44 was his trust,
He never fired fires, still fourteen bit the dust.

(CHORUS)

Baz Reeves
Black Law Man

Words and Music by:
Cecil Williams

Chorus:
He was a law-man's law-man, a legend of his time.
Thirty seven long years — he laid his life on the line.

Verse:
It was in July and the year was seventy five,
two hundred U.S. Marshalls were deputized.
"Law and order—!" he cried, "We'll turn this thing around,"
that old hangin' judge — had come to town.
One of the most famous of that breed was a black law-man
named Baz Reeves.

Copyright July 25, 1988 Rolla, MO.

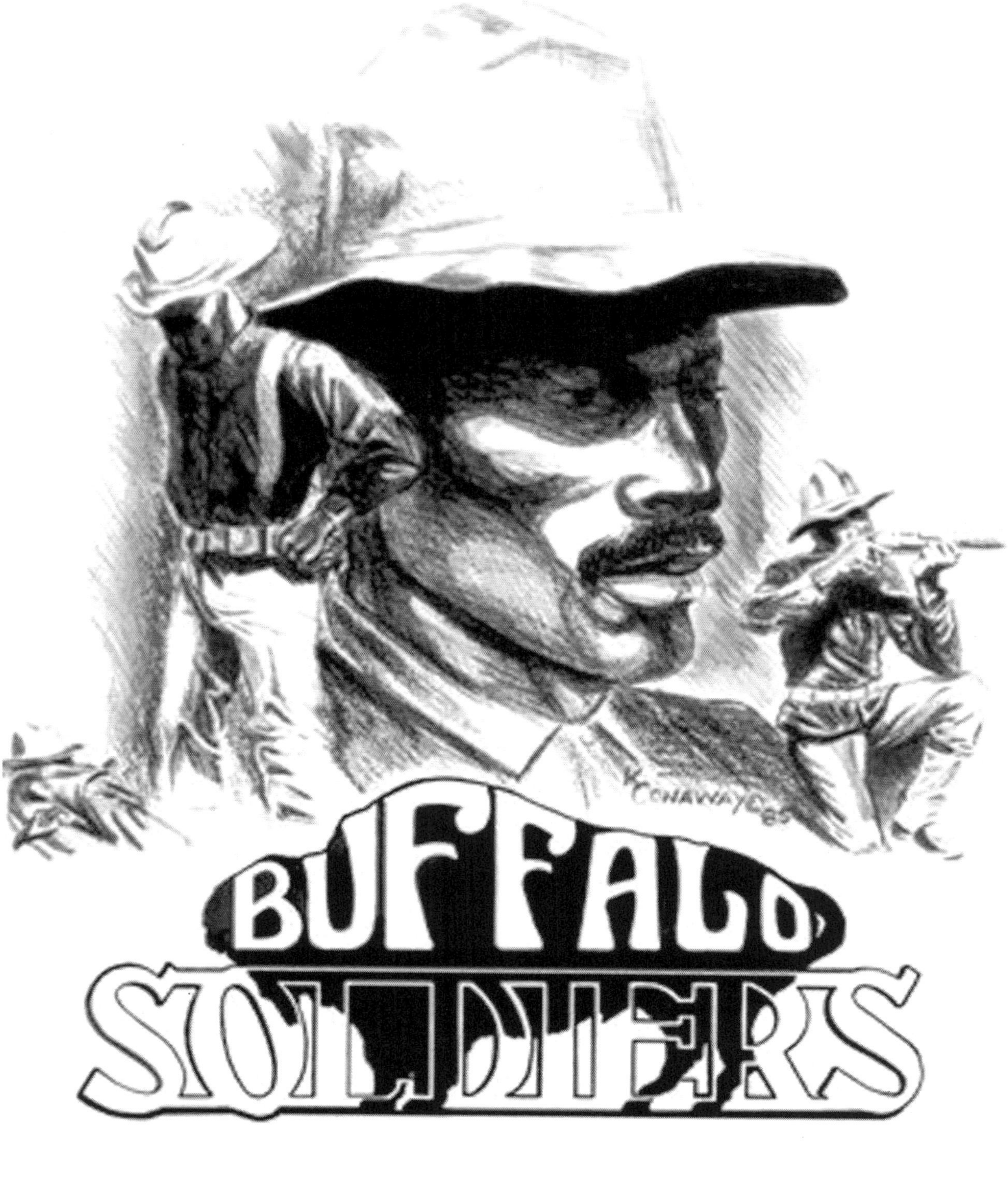
BUFFALO
SOLDIERS

Cavalrymen, Foot Soldiers, and Scouts

The Buffalo Soldiers

Friend and foe alike have honored the Buffalo Soldiers. Their name was given to them by their foes not only because their hair was like that of Buffalo and in winter campaigns they wore shaggy buffalo hide coats, but also because they fought with the bravery of the Buffalo, a sacred animal to the Indians. The Indians considered it bad medicine to scalp them.

Apparently the name Buffalo Soldier was applied at first to any black soldier on the western frontier. In time it became limited to cavalry troopers. Then when the Tenth Cavalry adopted its regimental coat-of-arms with a buffalo on it, that regiment seemed to have exclusive claim to the name. To white settlers and soldiers they were also known as "the brunettes," a name they didn't seem to resent, although they had greater pride in being called the Buffalo Soldiers.

Fairfax Downey in his 1941 book *Indian Fighting Army* was one of the first white historians to acknowledge the military ability and skill of the buffalo soldiers at a time in America when blacks in the military had been relegated to labor and fatigue duties.

> *Negroes, many of them fresh from slavery, served in this cosmopolitan army under white officers. Fine horsemen, hard fighters, well disciplined, they formed such splendid regiments as the 10th Cavalry. From their wooly hair and the shaggy hide coats they wore on winter campaigns, the Indians christened them "Buffalo Soldiers".* (24)

Colonel Benjamin Grierson, the first commander of the Tenth Cavalry, had led white troops on the six hundred-mile raid into Confederate territory that Grant "called the war's most brilliant foray." But for Grierson commanding the Buffalo Soldiers was the highlight of his career. He not only was their commanding officer, he was their father-confessor, lawyer, teacher, and link to their relatives back east.

Another of their officers, John J. Pershing, joined the Tenth as a shave-tail lieutenant. He became Black Jack Pershing early in his career in leading a company of Buffalo Soldiers against bandits and Indians in Montana. He commanded the regiment for ten years and led them in two of the last cavalry charges in military history against the Spanish at San Juan Hill and Pancho Villa in Mexico.

After he had commanded the Allied Expeditionary Forces in World War I, Pershing wrote about his days on the western frontier with the Tenth: "It has been an honor which I am proud to claim to have been one time a member of that intrepid organization of the Army which has added glory to the military history of America--the 10th Cavalry" (Katz 212).

Frederic Remington rode with both the Ninth and Tenth Cavalry and marched with the Twenty-fourth and Twenty-fifth Infantry. He was always astonished at their stamina in the field. One of his best known paintings, "Captain Dodge's Colored Troopers to the Rescue," presents the climax to a forced march to save white troops surrounded on the Milk River by the Ute Indians during the Ghost Dance uprising. On that occasion, the Ninth Cavalry rode one hundred miles in thirty hours to rescue the famed Seventh. Downey says about the ride of the Ninth relieving the Seventh:

> *On December 30, 1890, it [the 7th] fought a sharp engagement at White Clay Creek against odds heavy enough to make the arrival of a detachment of the 9th Cavalry extremely welcome. The black troopers of the 9th, who had a way of arriving at critical moments, galloped up behind Major Guy V. Henry, healed of his wounds and back to the wars. Their onset with three pack artillery howitzers clinched the victory. They had ridden 100 miles and taken part in two fights within thirty hours. (270)*

Calvary, Foot Soldiers, and Scouts: *The Buffalo Soldiers*

Private W. H. Prather, of Troop I on the Ninth wrote a ballad about the battle, which became a favorite among troops and settlers according to Downey. The chorus emphasizes the reputation of the Ninth among the Indians and the courage and bad luck of the Seventh.

> *The 9th marched out with splendid cheer the Bad Lands to explo'r--*
> *With Colonel Henry at their head they never fear the foe;*
> *So on they rode from Xmas even 'til dawn of Xmas day;*
> *They 9th is of courage bold, both officers and men,*
> *But bad luck seems to follow them and twice has took them in;*
> *They came in contact with Big Foot's warriors in their fierce might*
> *This chief made sure had a chance of vantage in the fight. (271-72)*

Shortly after the formation of the Tenth Cavalry it had performed a similar feat when it relieved the white troops at Beecher's Island in 1868. In the words of Tenth Cavalry trooper, Reuben Waller,

> *One great sensation as the rescue at Beecher Island, on the Arickare Creek, in Colorado, September, 1868. The Indians had surrounded General Forsyth and fifty brave men, and had killed and wounded twenty men, and had compelled the rest to live on dead horse flesh for nine days on a small island. Colonel L. H. Carpenter, with his Company H, Tenth U. S. Cavalry, was at Cheyenne Wells, Colorado, one hundred miles from Beecher Island. Jack Stillwell brought us word of the fix that Beecher was in and we entered the race for the island, and in twenty-six hours, Colonel Carpenter and myself, as his hostler, rode into the rifle pits. (Carroll 198)*

George Armstrong Custer also recognized the valor of the Buffalo Soldiers even though he refused to accept a command with them. His recognition comes indirectly from his wife's memoirs. Elizabeth Bacon Custer was writing to put her dead husband in the best possible light in her memoirs. In the first fight of the Seventh Cavalry at Fort Wallace, it was a dozen Buffalo soldiers on a supply mission who turned the tide at the height of Roman Nose's attack. Mrs. Custer wrote,

> *While the fight was going on, the two officers in command found themselves near each other on the skirmish line and observed a wagon with four mules tearing out to the line of battle. It was filled with Negroes, standing up, all firing in the direction of the Indians. The driver lashed the mules with the blacksnake and roared at them as they ran. When the skirmish line was reached, the colored men leaped out and began firing again. No one had ordered them to leave their picket station, but they were determined that no soldiering should be carried on in which their valor was not proved. (Carroll 189-90)*

The Black Ninth and Tenth Cavalry regiments became legends throughout the West. At one time in Texas, the Ninth was the only military presence to defend the settlers from bandits and Indians. Comprising twenty percent of the U. S. Cavalry, these regiments covered the area from the Mississippi to the Rockies, from Canada to Mexico. Occasionally they even crossed the Rio Grande in pursuit of Mexican or Indian raiders. They crossed into Mexico with Pershing in his campaign against Villa.

The Tenth developed its own military vocabulary. Veterans always referred to a trooper in his first enlistment as "young soldier" rather than recruit, the standard term used in the army. They also always used "sir" at least three times in responding to any order. For example, "Yes sir, lieutenant, sir, as ordered, sir."

Ironically they faced increasing discrimination from the white settlers they were defending. A Remington painting shows Buffalo Soldiers shooting in Bill Powell's saloon in Green County, Texas. His short story, "The Worm Turns," illustrates that the black troopers did not always accept quietly discrimination and prejudice from the whites.

Quite often, individual troopers had to desert to protect themselves from vigilante action by citizens. Still, of 10,939 desertions in 1867, only 3.6 percent were black. This is an amazing figure considering the level of prejudice

Calvary, Foot Soldiers, and Scouts: The Buffalo Soldiers

and the loneliness they faced. Most either did not have families or were separated from their families.

Sexual incidents did occur. Prostitutes were found at all frontier posts. General A. H. Terry, for instance, complained of the two brothels in Sturgis City, Dakota Territory, "catering to the taste and pandering to the passion of the colored troops, for they are 'stocked' with colored prostitutes--negresses and mulattos" (Thompson 231). Nevertheless, the rate of venereal disease among the black troopers apparently was no higher than among the whites.

The white prejudice and folklore about the sexual prowess of black men also was found in the army. At Fort Davis on November 21, 1872, an officer's wife shot a black trooper trying to climb through her bedroom window. All the whites assumed that the trooper was intent on rape. The first black officer in the army, Lieutenant Henry O. Flipper, believed that the real reason for his dismissal was that he had been too friendly with the wife of a white officer. Long after Flipper's death, President Clinton pardoned him in 1999. President Clinton recognized in granting the pardon that the court martial was unjust. Further, the President acknowledged the contributions Flipper made to his country, both as an officer and civilian.

Colonel George Andrews wrote of these sexual fears,

> *It is now seventeen months since I commenced my service with Colored Troops, and during that time attempts similar to the one related above have been made upon officers quarters at Fort Duncan, Stockton, and Davis, and I think McKavett and Concho. While stationed at Fort Clark, five such attempts were reported to me. (Thompson 232)*

As can be seen, much of Andrews' comments on attempted rapes are largely based on hearsay evidence and reflect the prevailing prejudices.

Frederic Remington, however, was a more objective witness to the activities of the black soldiers. Remington admired their bravery and tried to overcome white stereotypes.

> *They may be tired and they may be hungry, but they do not see fit to augment their misery by finding fault with everybody and everything. In this particular they are charming men with whom to serve. As to their bravery, I am often asked, 'Will they fight?' This is easily answered. They have fought many, many times. (69)*

He was quite right. Fourteen black soldiers were among the 419 Congressional Medal of Honor winners in the Indian Wars. He also observed that their relationships with their officers were closer than those of the white enlisted men. "In barracks, no soldier is allowed by his fellows to 'cuss out' a just and respected superior"(69).

Still, even Remington tended to stereotype their legendary handling of horses and mules. He wrote, "...the Negro cavalrymen carried on conversations with their horses. Strange people, but yet not half as strange as the Indians...."

Although the Twenty-fourth and Twenty-fifth Infantry Regiments are not remembered as glamorously in their activities as the cavalry regiments, they played an even more significant role in taming and building the West. They campaigned against the Apaches in the Southwest and against the Sioux in the Dakotas. They kept the homesteaders and the ranchers from fighting in cattle country. They built forts and roads, strung and repaired telegraph wires, provided escorts for stage and supply routes, guarded water holes and stage stations and provided all sorts of services for civilians.

The Twenty-fifth Infantry built rock-walled roadbeds leading to Fort Davis that still stand. Their regimental history describes their duty in Texas as "a continuous series of building and repairing military posts, roads and telegraph lines; of escort and guard duty of all descriptions; of marching and counter-marching from post to post and of scouting for Indians which resulted in a few unimportant skirmishes" (Thompson 219-220).

But there was time for pride in belonging to the army. Every evening except Saturday, Fort Davis had a dress parade. All the families of officers, enlisted, and civilians came out to watch the precision of the Buffalo Soldiers in their dress uniforms. These black soldiers provided moments of patriotism and entertainment at a post that offered little relief from the hardship of the frontier.

Calvary, Foot Soldiers, and Scouts: The Buffalo Soldiers

The Twenty-fifth Infantry regimental band became extremely popular with the citizens of the Dakota and Montana Territories. In Missoula they performed on all holidays and patriotic occasions and gave regular concerts on Thursday evenings. Their popularity as musicians probably caused the black infantry to have better relations with the whites of the territories than the cavalry.

Still there were incidents of friction between the two races. Nevertheless, perhaps because of their music, as Fowler believes, or perhaps because the infantry was less mobile and became more a part of the community where they were stationed than the cavalry, the Twenty-fourth and Twenty-fifth Infantry Regiments did not experience extreme prejudice.

Porter summarizes the service of the black regiments on the western frontier in the following way:

> *For a quarter-century these regiments served without intermission against hostile Cheyenne, Comanche, Kiowa, Apache and Utes, and against Mexican outlaws and border desperadoes, taking part in nearly 200 engagements, major and minor. More than once detachments from these regiments came to the aid of white troops in desperate straits. For months and years at a time and garrisons of many frontier posts consisted of detachments from Negro regiments and their white officers. The campaigns against the Apache chiefs Victorio and Nana--more importantly actually than those against the more publicized Geronimo--were conducted almost entirely by Negro troopers. The quality of their service is indicated by the fact that during 1870-1890 fourteen Negro soldiers won the prestigious Medal of Honor, while several others received Certificates of Merit. (470)*

Why did they serve a country that treated them as second class citizens? Why did they defend settlers who viewed them with prejudice and practiced discrimination against them? Why did they serve in an army that would not allow them to be officers?

Nations have historically depended on the economically deprived for their armies. The British had enlisted its army from the poor of England, Ireland, and Scotland who served for the king's coin. Many immigrants from Europe to the United States found the army on the frontier as a way to support themselves.

But blacks saw in the army more than just an economic opportunity. Don Rickey believes most joined the army for social as well as economic reasons. Most blacks, as well as most whites, were illiterate when they enlisted. The army had a policy that all enlisted men should be given an elementary education. There were a variety of attempts and successes in the schools at frontier posts to teach reading and writing. Among the most successful schools to teach blacks was the one that the black chaplain, Colonel Allen Allensworth, established at Fort Bayard, N. M.

As Katz has written,

> *In an age that viewed black men as either comic or dangerous, and steadily reduced the decent jobs open to them, army life offered more dignity than almost anything civilian had to offer. In the army they could live surrounded by those symbols by which man has traditionally cushioned a lowly status--pride in country, decent clothes, discipline, skill development, and loyalty to others. If any of these men felt they were mercenaries hired by whites to crush red men there is no evidence of this in the historical literature. (201)*

It could be that the black troopers were emulating white values in considering the red men inferior. They may have sought too zealously full American citizenship by engaging in the frontier wars to make the West safe for whites. It is more likely, however, they joined the army for individual opportunities even though they knew they would have no chance to become commissioned officers. They knew their equipment and horses were always rejects from the white regiments. While the Seventh Cavalry and the other white regiments had silk regimental flags, the Buffalo on the homemade flag of the Tenth cavalry became a symbol of military pride for the United States Army.

Ironically, a former Confederate, General Joseph Wheeler, led them in their first overseas engagement at San Juan Hill during the Spanish American War. Wheeler, one of the South's finest cavalry officers during the Civil War, led a

Calvary, Foot Soldiers, and Scouts: The Buffalo Soldiers

squadron from the Ninth and Tenth Cavalry on foot in the charge on July 1, 1898.

Theodore Roosevelt, commanding the Rough Riders who gained all the credit for the victorious charge, recalled that day in a speech in October, 1898.

> *We went up absolutely intermingled, so that no one could tell whether it was the Rough Riders or the men of the 9th who came forward with the greater courage to offer their lives in the service of their country... When you've been under fire with a man and fought side by side with him, and eaten with him when you had anything to eat, and hungered with him when you hadn't, you felt sort of a comradeship that you don't feel for any man that you have associated with in other ways. (Drotning, 144)*

Other officers in the Cuban campaign recognized that the black troops as members of the regular army conducted themselves better than the white volunteers. One white office said,

> *If it had not been for the Negro cavalry the Rough Riders would have been exterminated. I am not a Negro lover. My father fought with Mosby's Rangers, and I was born in the South, but the Negroes saved that fight, and the day will come when General Shafter [the commander of the American expeditionary force in Cuba] will give them credit for their bravery. (Drotning, 151)*

Another southern officer recalled, "I never saw such fighting as those Tenth Cavalry men did. They didn't seem to know what fear was, and their battle hymn was 'There'll be a hot time in the old town tonight.'" (Drotning, 151)

Only a short time later, however, when he was campaigning for the presidency, Roosevelt seems to have forgotten the black troopers who fought so valiantly in Cuba and saved the Rough Riders from annihilation at San Juan Hill. American society became even more segregated with the twentieth century. All American office seekers, including Roosevelt, made their appeals to white voters who did not want to hear about black heroes.

L. D. Reddick called the years from 1866 to 1900 the "Golden Day" for black soldiers. Prejudice in the 20th century caused segregated units of blacks to be used as labor battalions in France in World War I and looked on as unreliable soldiers in World War II. Their glorious record on the western frontiers against bandits, Indians, and outlaws had been forgotten or intentionally put aside.

Yet perhaps Captain Harry Truman's western background as the man from Independence and his service with Black Jack Pershing in France caused him to remember the valor of the Buffalo Soldiers. As President in 1948 Truman ordered the desegregation of the army. In 1867 the Twenty-fourth Infantry Regiment had been the first black military unit to meet the enemy on the western frontier. In July, 1950, they became the last segregated combat unit in the Korean War.

"Buffalo Soldiers"

El Caney, Santiago.
And the charge up San Juan hill.
Rough riders, Teddy's fighters,
But those Buffalo Soldiers were there.

I'll share with you their legend
By now you ought to know,
About that group of soldiers,
Named after the sacred buffalo.

(CHORUS)

Buffalo Soldiers,
Ninth and Tenth Cavalry,
Buffalo Soldiers,
Twenty-Fourth and Twenty-Fifth Infantry.
Many years have come and gone,
Since they wore their Yankee Blue,
Though their deeds linger on,
Still today as strong as true.
From the banks of the Rio Grande,
To the North Dakota land.
From the plains of ol' Oklahoma,
Westward ho! across burning sand.

We opposed our red-skinned brothers,
And they fought to the bitter end,
They were brave and courageous warriors,
None more gallant fighting men.

Apache, Kiowa, Commanche,
Cheyenne and the mighty Sioux,
Apache, Kiowa, Commanche,
Cheyenne and the might Sioux.

Throughout our country's history,
Many brave men have fought and died,
Throughout this land of the free,
Many broken hearted mothers have cried

On God's green earth you'll never find,
No greater breed of mankind.
Now all we seek as mortal men,
Is freedom to be our own men.

Buffalo Soldiers,
May your banner be held high.
Buffalo Soldier,
May your legend never die.

(CHORUS)

Buffalo Soldiers

Words and Music by:
 Cecil Williams

El Ca-ney - San-ti-a-go and the charge up San Juan hill, Rough Ri-ders, Ted-dy's figh-ters but those Buf-fa-lo Sol-diers were there. I'll share with you their le-gend, by now you ought to know, a-bout that group of sol-diers named af-ter the sa-cred buf-fa-lo.

Chorus:

Buf-fa-lo Sol-diers, ninth and tenth ca-val-ry

Buf-fa-lo Sol-diers twen-ty fourth and twen-ty fifth in-fan-try.

to next verse:

Copyright October 9, 1988 Rolla, MO.

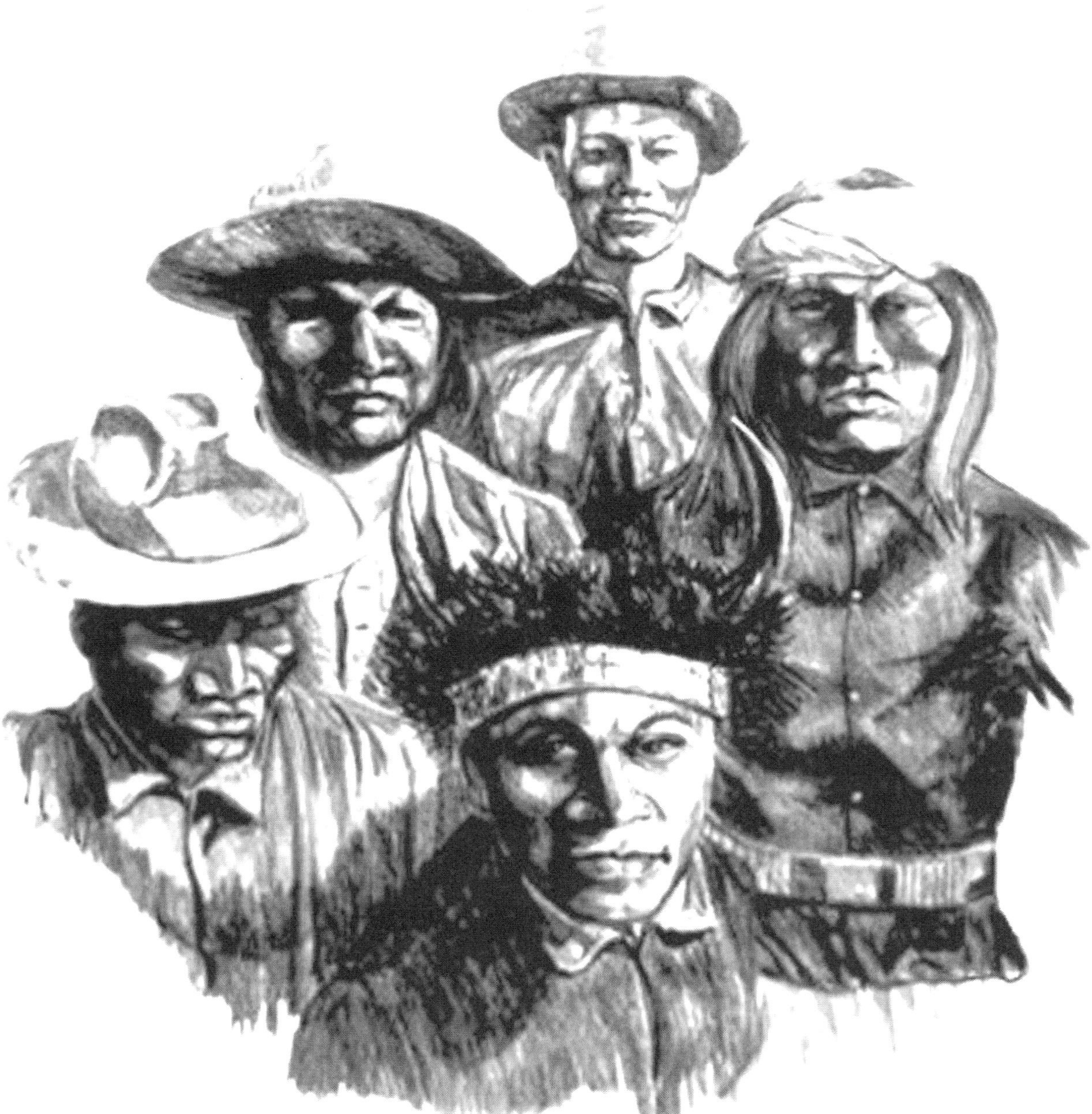

The Black Seminole Indian Scouts

Kenneth W. Porter states,

> *The Seminole Scouts and their leader were not, of course, by any means wholly responsible for achieving permanent cessation of Indian raids on the Texas frontier. Regular United States troops had played an important part, but without the scouts the work of the regular troops would to a large degree have been futile. (490)*

To many military historians the Black Seminole Indian Scouts were the greatest fighting unit to ever be assembled in the United States Army. By 1882, they had helped bring law and order to the brutal border between Texas and Mexico. They had engaged in twenty-six expeditions, twelve major battles, and numerous skirmishes without losing a single man. They had only one man seriously injured in their eleven-year history. Four of the fifty-man unit had won the Congressional Medal of Honor.

Texans honored their white commander, Lieutenant John L. Bullis, with the title "The Friend of the Frontier." The people of West Texas called him and his command the "Thunderbolt of the Texas Frontier." They gave him a sword in 1881 with the following inscriptions: on one side, "Presented to Jno. L. Bullis by the people of West Texas;" and on the other side, "He protected our homes-- our homes are open to him." Kinney County also gave him a sword engraved with the words: "Presented by the People of Kinney County as a token of their undying gratitude."

The Texas legislature on April 7, 1882, passed a resolution that read,

> *We tender our sincere thanks in the name of the people of this state, to Lieutenant J. L. Bullis, of the Twenty-fourth Infantry, United States Army, for the gallant and efficient services rendered by him and his command in behalf of the people of the frontier of this State,*

in repelling the depredations of Indians and other enemies of the frontier of Texas. (Wallace 84)

Many called him "the greatest Indian fighter in the history of the United States Army" (Porter 490). Almost his entire military career from the time he was commissioned a captain in the Civil War was as an officer of black troops. After the Civil War he was a second lieutenant with the 24th Infantry (the Buffalo Soldiers) on the Texas frontier. On September 1, 1871, he and four privates of Company H, 9th Cavalry, attacked twenty-eight Indians, fought them for nearly an hour, and retreated with a herd of 200 Indian cattle (Wallace 77).

Then he became commander of the Seminole Scouts. Together in nine years from 1873 to 1881, Bullis and his scouts participated in twenty-six expeditions, fighting in some engagements when they were outnumbered six or eight to one.

The scouts were disbanded in 1914 and forgotten by the Army. One of the Medal of Honor recipients, Pompey Factor, in 1926 was denied an army pension on the basis that there was no record of his service. Who were these remarkable fighting men?

Their history began in Alabama, Georgia, and Florida when runaway slaves and free blacks lived as Black Seminole Indians before the Seminole Wars. Andrew Jackson, as President, forced their removal to Oklahoma with the other Seminoles.

Soon the Black Seminoles became discontent with reservation life and immigrated to Mexico where they became renowned as Indian fighters for Santa Anna. Their reputation as trackers and fighters was so high that Major Zenas R. Bliss, then commanding the 25th United States Cavalry, sent Major Frank W. Perry to Nacimento, Mexico, to recruit them in 1870.

In what the Scouts and their families called "de treaty" or "de treatment," they were promised payments of their expenses in returning to the United States, monthly wages, provisions for their families, and grants of land if they would serve the United States Army as scouts along the Texas border. They also were to be supplied with arms, ammunition, and rations, and were to be compensated for supplying their own horses. In Mexico, they had been using muzzle-loaded rifles, but the Army equipped them first with Spencer carbines, and shortly thereafter, the Sharps, a much-improved rifle.

Calvary, Foot Soldiers, and Scouts: The Black Seminole Indian Scouts

Although the treaty between the government and the Scouts was apparently never written down, the Army did meet the terms of its agreement except for the grant of land. Throughout their service they continued to petition for land. Both the Army and the Department of Interior denied that they had any land to give.

This continued to be a point of contention between them and the government. Throughout their history they were forced to be squatters on land to make a living when the Army cut their rations or whenever Congress reduced the military budget.

Chief John Horse, their leader, made many pleas for this part of their contract to be honored. Many white officers, including General Phil Sheridan supported him in his pleas. In the end, John Horse, who had parleyed with Presidents Taylor and Polk during the Seminole Wars and served American Presidents from 1870-1882, returned to Mexico to look for land for his people. He was never seen again.

While the United States did not fully honor its part of the treaty, the Black Seminole Scouts certainly gave full service to honor their part. Despite being frequently harassed and attacked by white Texans they were protecting from Indian raids, they were almost on constant patrol. From the beginning they were an unconventional army unit, particularly in dress. Many had adopted the Indian style of dress down to war bonnets or buffalo horns. As seasoned fighters, they were not interested in army drill and routine.

Lieutenant Bullis understood this and understood them. Their loyalty seems to be more to him and the honor of their unit than anything else. Their intense loyalty to Bullis was shown dramatically when he and three scouts attacked twenty-five to thirty Comanches near Eagle's Nest Crossing of the Pecos. In the fight, Bullis lost his horse as they retreated.

Sergeant John Ward turned back when he saw his commander on foot and shouted to the other two, "We can't leave the lieutenant, boys." The three scouts, firing their weapons, rode back to him. Ward's carbine sling was cut by one bullet from the Indians and another broke his carbine stock. He rode to Bullis, helped him mount behind him, and the four men escaped with their lives. The three scouts were awarded the Congressional Medal of Honor for their bravery that day.

Attacking their enemy when they were out-numbered was not unusual for the Seminole Scouts. This was one of the qualities they admired most in their commander. John Phillips, one of the Scouts, said about Bullis,

> *The Scouts thought a lot of Bullis. Lieutenant Bullis was the only officer ever did stay the longest with us. That fella suffer just like we-all out in de woods. He was a good man. He was a Injun fighter. He was tuff. He didn't care how big a bunch dey was, he went into em every time, but he look for his men. His men was on equality, too. He didn't stand and say, "Go yonder"; he would say "Come on boys, lets go get 'em." (Katz 235)*

They were able to campaign effectively against the Indian raiders because they could live off the land, move rapidly, stay in the field months at a time, and track their enemy through any kind of terrain. Bullis became known as a "tireless marcher." The Comanches called him the Whirlwind and the Thunderbolt. He and his men could live by eating rattlesnakes when no other game was available. A luxurious ration for Bullis and the Scouts was a can of corn for a march. Troopers tell that he had a rule that they should live on one can of food a day, whether it was corned beef or peaches.

Bullis endured the same hardships his men did and became to them more of a family member than a commander. He visited them in their home camps often, performing marriages and giving congratulations when children were born. He also had time for a family of his own. He had married Alice Rodriguez in 1872, but she died in 1887. He married Josephine Withers in 1891, and they had three daughters.

Bullis and his scouts became legendary throughout the Southwest in their exploits. Sometimes, they served with regular cavalry units including white regiments and the Buffalo Soldiers. Usually they operated independently in small bands.

For instance, on the night of October 16, 1875, Bullis and Sergeant Miller took thirty horses and mules from hostile Indians at their camp at Laguna Sabinas. In 1876 in a major engagement, Bullis, with twenty scouts, and twenty black cavalrymen and one other officer, engaged the Lipan Indians near Saragossa, Mexico. In a half hour of hand-to-hand combat, fourteen Indians

Calvary, Foot Soldiers, and Scouts: *The Black Seminole Indian Scouts*

were killed, while not a single American soldier was killed or wounded even though they were outnumbered.

The fact that in all their Indian engagements not a single Black Seminole Scout lost his life caused the older generation of scouts to think of themselves as having divine protection. Bill Daniels said, "When you are fighting for the right and have your trust in God, he will spread his hand over you"(Porter 485). Of course, much of what they were fighting for was the land the American government promised but never gave.

Even though they were fortunate never to lose a man in their Indian campaigns, they were not so fortunate in dealing with outlaws, particularly the notorious "King" Fisher. Fisher boasted that he had killed a man for every year of his life, not counting Mexicans. In a saloon fight with Fisher and his gang, the scouts suffered their first fatal casualty when Chief John Horse's nephew, Corporal George Washington was shot in the stomach. He died several months later from his wound.

Then in Kinney County, Fisher and his men were apparently hired to drive the scouts out. Chief Horse was ambushed and wounded while his companion Titus Payne was killed. Another incident in the following year occurred when the Kinney County sheriff shot Adam Payne in the back at such close range that his clothes caught on fire.

Three killings by whites in less than two years caused five of the scouts to return to Mexico where they joined Colonel Pedro Avincular Valdez to continue Indian fighting. Still most of the scouts remained loyal and stayed with the army to protect the border.

In the next few years they engaged in epic feats of tracking and fighting, constantly in the field, and several times crossing into Mexico in pursuit of hostiles. One of those epic campaigns was in 1879, when they tracked Mescalero raiders across the desert for thirty-four days with little water. On one occasion, when they were almost dying of thirst, Sergeant David Bowlegs showed his knowledge of the desert by finding a "sleeping spring." Digging beneath the sand he made the water flow again. Finally they trailed the raiders to the Fort Stanton, New Mexico, reservation. There the Indian agent would not surrender them. In that campaign they had been in the field eighty days and had journeyed 12,666 miles.

The Black West in Story and Song

On April 14, 1881, a band of Lipans raided Texas soil on the headwaters of the Rio Frio, killing Mrs. McLauren and a child, Allen Reiss. This was the last important Indian raid in Texas and the last major Indian battle for the scouts. Two weeks after the raid the Seminole Scouts were ordered to track the raiders. They found the cold trail even though the Indians had "killed a horse and made shoes out of the rawhide so they wouldn't make tracks"(Porter 489). On May 2 they attacked the camp, killing four warriors, mortally wounding their chief, who escaped, and capturing a squaw, a child, and twenty-one horses and mules.

The following year, 1882, the Seminole Scouts made twelve expeditions into the field, covered 3,662 miles, and found no sign of Indian raiders. For all practical purposes, the settlers' fears of Indian raids had ended in Texas. Of course, the Seminole Scouts were not alone in bringing an end to the raids along the border. Nevertheless, as Porter has written, "Texas in large measure owed her final exemption from such Indian raids" to the Black Seminole Scouts (490).

In a time of relative peace, Bullis became an Indian agent on the Apache reservation near San Carlos, Arizona. In 1893, he became an agent for the Pueblo and Jicarilla Indians in New Mexico. In 1897, the army appointed him paymaster with the rank of major in San Antonio. He served in the Spanish-American War in Cuba and the Philippines, and in 1904 he retired with the rank of brigadier general.

In return for their service, the scouts were gradually reduced in number, evicted from their homes on the Fort Clark reservations, and in 1914 disbanded. Their folklore contains a story about Bullis, now a general and dying of a heart attack, resisting the disbanding of his old unit. John Jefferson, one of the scouts, says that Bullis was ill in his home when the news of the order to disband reached him. According to Jefferson, he immediately got out of bed, started to dress. His nurse protested, "General, what are you doing out of bed? Don't you realize that you are a sick man?" "Colonel _____ says he's going to disband my old scouts," the general replied. "I'm going to Fort Clark and stop him." According to the story, Bullis then collapsed and died.

Calvary, Foot Soldiers, and Scouts: The Black Seminole Indian Scouts

This story doesn't fit the facts, however. Bullis collapsed and died of a heart attack at a boxing match in San Antonio on May 26, 1911. The final order to disband did not come until three years later, July 10, 1914. But the story shows the scouts continued admiration for Bullis and their belief the unit would never have been disbanded if he had lived.

In December, 1917, a new military camp north of San Antonio was named for him. The Seminole Scouts became lost in American history and only a faded memory to the descendants of the West Texans who honored them as the saviors of the frontier.

"The Black Seminoles/Black Seminole Scouts"

We know the story of Texas and the
men of the Alamo, and yet there's another
breed just as brave and bold.
This is the story of thirty brave
souls, this is the saga of the Black Seminoles

Runaways from Georgia sought freedom in
the everglades. Send 'em back Jackson said
those are runaway slaves,
Osceola told Jackson no slaves on Seminole
land, They are free to stay as long as I say
stay on Seminole land!

Send 'em back 'ol Jackson said, Or I'll
send in my troops, We'll bust you
down and drag away those runaways to boot!
Fight they did tooth and claw, Saber,
Battle ax, Bow and Arrow, Musket,
Bowie Knife and Tomahawk!

(CHORUS)

Good 'ol Boys battling the Black and Red,
Fighting and dying, Swamp water turned Red.
The Dragoons didn't beat 'em, They didn't
give in. It was over a hundred years before it
did end! Four swamp wars were fought!

Civil War ended, unfinished business,
Border trouble, Renegades, Texas Outlaws.
Needed some one to track 'em
Black Seminole Scouts of the Black
Seminole Tribe. Find them!
Thirty Brave souls rode up from
Old Mexico!

(CHORUS)

They could ride like Mexicans, Track like Indians,
fight like the Devil and Shoot like Tennesseans!
Remember the Alamo! Remember the Legend
of the Black Seminoles!

Black Seminole Scouts

Words and Music by:
Cecil Williams

We know the story of Texas and the men of the Alamo, and and yet there's another breed just as brave and as bold. this is the story of thirty brave souls -. this is the saga of the Black-Seminoles -, runaways from Georgia sought freedom in the Everglades. "Send 'em back," said Jackson, "those are runaway slaves."

Chorus:

Good ol' boys a battlin' - the black and the red, fightin' and dyin', swamp water turnin' red - -.

to next verse:

Copyright November 13, 1989   Rolla, MO.

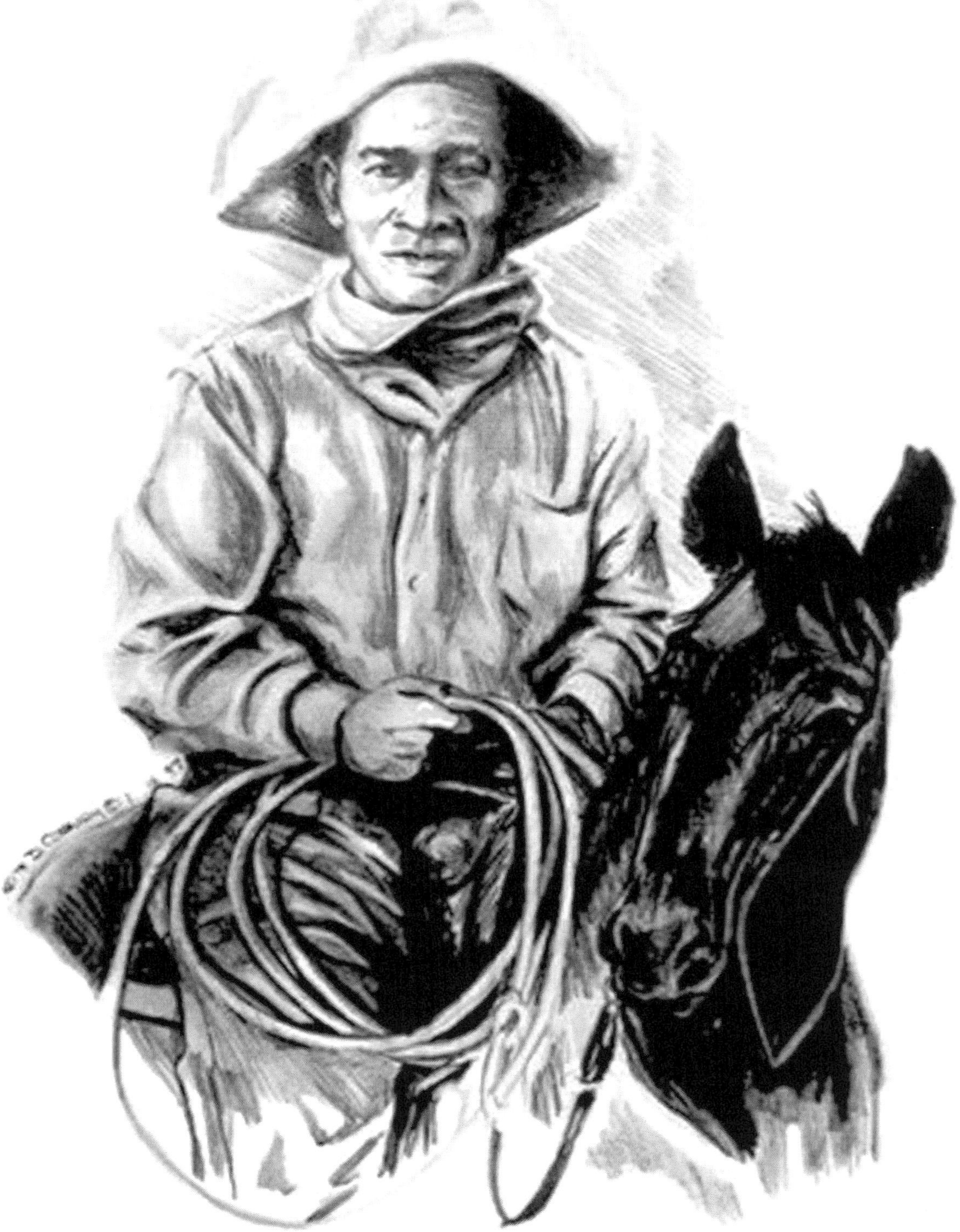

Cowboys, Ranchers, and Riders

80 John Wallace

Just as any boy, Daniel Webster Wallace dreamed of being a cowboy. He even dared to dream that he would be a rancher. But he never dreamed he would become one of the largest landowners in Texas.

Born a slave in Victoria County, Texas, on September 15, 1860, he was always a dreamer. After the Civil War, he was able to go to school. To keep his attention in school, the teacher would send him outside for wood. Often he felt that he was asked to go get wood more than any of the other boys. Sometimes he would become sullen about carrying wood. Then the teacher would switch him or have him stand in the corner on one foot with a dunce cap on. Still, he kept his dreams.

Some of the people on the O'Daniel plantation where he was born and raised thought he was a lazy child even though he was big for his age and could chop cotton and plow all day as well as any one. Others thought of him as listless or even stupid because in the field he would chop with one hand, lean on his hoe frequently, and seek the shade whenever he could. Still he earned thirty to fifty cents a day and saved what he could because he knew his dream was coming true soon.

He had heard a cattle drive was starting west and he planned to join it. At three-thirty in the morning, he sneaked out of his mother's house and ran toward the sound of the cattle lowing.

Out of breath when he reached the herd, he asked the first man he saw to let him go with them. The trail boss told him they didn't need any more cowboys, but they did need a wrangler.

To fulfill his dream, Webster lied for one of the few times in his life. He had never been on any horse except the slow plow horses and mules of the plantation. He told the trail boss he could ride anything.

The boss told him to mount one of the cow ponies. At first the pony just stood there. In the saddle Webster waited for instructions. Then the pony began to buck while Webster held on to the horn and tried to keep his feet in the stirrups. The boss remembered when he was a tenderfoot and forced to ride a wild pony. He seized the bridle to quiet Webster's horse before it threw him.

With that Daniel Webster Wallace was a wrangler and made his first trail drive to Coleman County, Texas. For his first job as a cowboy he earned fifteen silver dollars, much more than he had ever made chopping cotton.

His next job was as a range cowboy for Sam Gholson, the famous Indian fighter. Because there were no fences, this job required him to range up to a hundred miles looking for mavericks and strays.

Now with more experience with horses, he became a horse breaker and wrangler for the outfit. Horses could lie down on him, throw him over their ears, and buck him off, but his courage never faltered. He would always say to the other cowboys, "Bring him back; let me try him again," no matter how wild the horse was.

As wrangler he was the first up in the morning and the last in bed at night because he was responsible for the remuda. Every morning he had to ride those horses that still bucked to smooth them out so the cowboys wouldn't have any trouble with them on the range.

His boss, Sam Gholson, moved to a new free range six months after Webster went to work for him. So he went to work for the Nunn ranch, one of the largest in the area, with eight thousand head of cattle.

Comanches were raiding the Nunn herds then. It was common for them to make quick attacks both night and day. One day when Webster and some other cowboys were farther from camp than they planned, a small band of Indians surprised them. All of the cowboys except one left their horses and hid behind trees and rocks. The cowboy who tried to make a run for it was captured and killed. Those who had hidden escaped.

Webster also had to face prejudice on the range. Once during roundup a bully from a neighboring ranch bragged on what he did to "cowboys of color." Webster could take only so much verbal abuse and then began to return the insults. The bully drew a line in the dirt and dared him to cross it.

Although he stood six feet three, Webster would never strike the first blow in a fight out of the principles he had learned from his mother. After the bully struck the first blow, he became a whirlwind and the fight was soon over. With

Cowboys, Ranchers, and Riders: *80 John Wallace*

all the fight taken out of him, the bully rose from the ground and offered Webster his hand. With that, following the code of the range, they became fast friends.

Webster was also a good roper. One day he accepted the challenge of roping a buffalo from his horse. A foolish act. This time he almost lost his life before he could cut the rope. He learned buffaloes are too strong for a cowboy to rope.

He was ready to accept any challenge the range or cowboys presented. However, he was not ready to follow the life of most cowboys when they went to town. While other riders were gambling, drinking, and whoring, Webster was saving his money. The ranch owner, Mr. Nunn, was a devout man who did not allow cursing and vulgar language in his presence. Webster took him as a role model.

He always remembered the teachings of his mother. Upon hearing that his mother was ill, he rode a month back home to Victoria County to see her again. But she died before he could reach home. He was now seventeen; his ties to Victoria County were cut, and he was a full-fledged cowboy.

He had heard that Clay Mann needed hands on his ranch. Needing a job, he rode four hundred miles through Indian country to Buffalo Gap, on the border of Runnels and Taylor Counties to the Mann Ranch. Mann's brand was "80," which was burned from the backbone to the belly on the sides of his cattle. Webster's long association with this ranch and his close relationship with Clay Mann earned him the name 80 John Wallace.

80 John soon became famous in cattle country for his ability to estimate the size of a herd of cattle. Once when Mann and a visiting rancher argued over the number of cattle in the herd, they decided to bet on the exact number. The rancher guessed 2000. 80 John set the figure at between 1775 and 1800. The tally that evening showed 1800 was very close, and Mann was declared the winner of the bet.

Mann trusted 80 John in every way. When he said, "I will do my best," Mann knew he could count on him. On one occasion Mann sent $30,000 in cash to the Cross Tie Ranch near Midland on wagon with 80 John in charge. At night he slept with the money under his head and delivered it after the three days' journey. Often when Mann had to be away from the ranch for extended periods, he left 80 John there to guard his wife and children.

The Black West in Story and Song

Mann and 80 John respected one another so much that they had an agreement that the cowboy would be paid only $125 of the $720 he earned for two years. At the end of two years, 80 John paid six hundred dollars for some cattle that Mann agreed could graze on his ranch. At the roundup that year those with the 80 brand and those with the word "Wallace" branded on them were driven to market together. Mann paid 80 John his share of the sale. With this sale, 80 John was on his way to becoming a rancher.

He continued to follow the advice of Mann and the teachings of Nunn and his mother to save his money. In 1885 he homesteaded and purchased two sections of land in Mitchell County. Having been too much of a dreamer as a boy to succeed in school, he now recognized as a landowner the importance of knowing how to read, write, and do arithmetic.

He enrolled in the second grade at Navarro County School for Negroes when he was twenty-five years old. He spent two winters there, and returned to ranch work in the summers. While his methods of calculating interest and measuring land remained unorthodox throughout his life, he apparently never forgot anything he was ever taught.

In Navarro County, he and a friend bought twelve acres to plant cotton. One spring morning 80 John plowed one row and the dreams of cowboy life returned. He left that morning and did not see that farm again for twenty years.

In Navarro County he did fulfill another of his dreams when he met Laura Dee Owen. She gave up her dreams of being a teacher and married Daniel Webster Wallace on April 8, 1888. Their first home was on one of Clay Mann's West Texas ranches.

When Mann died in 1889, 80 John continued to work for Mrs. Mann. One of his responsibilities was teaching the Mann boys riding, roping, and ranching. After fourteen years of working for the Manns, he decided to work for himself.

For a short while, he was a partner with Dave Roberson, another African-American rancher, but both were rugged individuals who wanted their own spreads. He began buying Durham cattle and keeping a large number of heifers to replace cull cows. As the years passed he acquired more cattle, more horses and more land.

Cowboys, Ranchers, and Riders: *80 John Wallace*

During this period he joined the newly formed Texas Southwestern Cattle Raisers' Association. He became highly respected by cattlemen of all races. One anecdote illustrates that for cattlemen there was no color line when it came to 80 John Wallace.

Trains were then segregated in Texas. One year 80 John was riding in the Jim Crow car on his way to the Cattlemen's Association in Fort Worth. Several white cattlemen were with him in the segregated "colored" car of the train enjoying their conversation with their old friend. The conductor told them they would have to move to the white car. One white rancher told him, "I have known 80 John for thirty years. We ate and slept on the ground together. I see no reason that makes it impossible for me to sit here now"(Branch 39). So for that day at least, the car was integrated.

The hospitality of the Wallace ranch was known throughout Texas and also knew no racial barriers. The doors of the Wallace house were never locked. People of all races came to feed their teams, to sleep, to enjoy good food and good company. The descendants of the O'Daniels, the family who had once owned Daniel Webster Wallace before emancipation, often spent the night when they visited in the area.

80 John Wallace continued to expand his land holdings and improve his stock. By the Great Depression in 1929, he owned fourteen and one half sections of land and six hundred head of cattle with no loan or mortgage or past due taxes on any of his property.

He was known during these dark economic times for his generosity to all-- red, white, and black. His tenants always received one third more than they estimated they would need to raise their crops to cover their monthly expenses before harvest time. He always bought from the lame and the blind whatever they were selling and then returned it to them for them to sell again.

Friends who were about to lose their homes received assistance. He wrote notes on these loans that protected the borrower from foreclosure.

Although he had little formal education himself, he emphasized the importance of education for all. He helped several needy students through college. The D. W. Wallace School for Negro Children in Colorado City, Texas, was named in his honor. He contributed to the building of the Baptist Church in Loraine, Texas, even though he belonged to another church, because African-American children could use the building for a school.

In his final illness, he had one more dream. He told his wife of fifty-one years, when she heard a mysterious voice call, "Three months from now you will know who called." Three months later he told her, "I'm going to leave you. It is just as natural to die as it is to live. Do the best you can. Sing 'On Jordan's Banks I Stand'" (Branch 51).

Hearing that he was ill, numerous old friends came to see him. Mrs. C. M. Mann, the wife of Clay Mann's son, visited frequently. M. H. O'Daniel, the son of the O'Daniels who owned the plantation where 80 John was born, came.

Despite his weakness, he entertained his friends and reviewed his business with the administrator of his estate. He outlined plans for the future with his family, but told them he would not be there. He told his children to treat one another right and always treat everyone right.

He told his wife, "I have reviewed my life from six years [old] until now--I have harmed no man, I am ready to go; what do you think of me?"

Kissing him, she answered, "You have always been my ideal, don't you know?" (Branch 51)

Then early on the morning of March 28, 1939, he had his final dream. He told his wife with a smile on his face, "'Don't you see her? She is calling me, she doing like this,' as he waved his hand as if someone beckoned to him" (Branch 52).

Then he died at the age of 79. People of all races in West Texas mourned him. Cattlemen and farmers from all over the state came to his funeral. As his daughter wrote about his death, "The old-time cattlemen did not have to sit on the front seat to hear what the minister was saying about the virtues of his life--they knew" (Branch 52).

"Daniel Webster Wallace"
(80 John)

This is the saga of a young cowhand,
Born a slave, Grew up a man.

A rancher in Texas was a
boyhood dream.
Hit the dusty trail at only fifteen.

Born Daniel Webster Wallace!
They called him 80 John!
Out in west Texas, He was
a native son.

80 John! 80 John!
Your story must be told,
To save a boy! To save
a girl! To save a lost soul.

He strived to do his very
best, Withstood every test.
Held fast to his boyhood dream,
A man of high esteem.

**It's good to dream
my friends, So hard to
make them real.**

Blood and sweat, Grit
and guts. Sometimes
there's gonna be tears.
(hang in there)

Your brand you left on
Texas, and a legacy in gold.
To save a boy, To save
girl to save a lost soul.

80 John! 80 John!
Your story must be
told. To save a boy
to save a girl,
try and save a lost
soul, (yeah)

Daniel Webster Wallace
"80 John"

Words and Music by:
 Cecil Williams

This is the sa - ga of a young cow - hand.

Born a slave, grew up a man. A ranch - er in Tex - as was a boy - hood dream -. Hit the dus - ty trail at on - ly fif - teen -. Dan - iel Web - ster Wal - lace, they called him Eigh - ty John. Out in west Tex - as, he was a na - tive son.

Chorus:

Eigh - ty John! Eigh - ty John -! Your sto - ry must be told. To save a boy, to save a girl, to save a lost soul.

Copyright November 18, 1991 Rolla, MO.

to next verse:

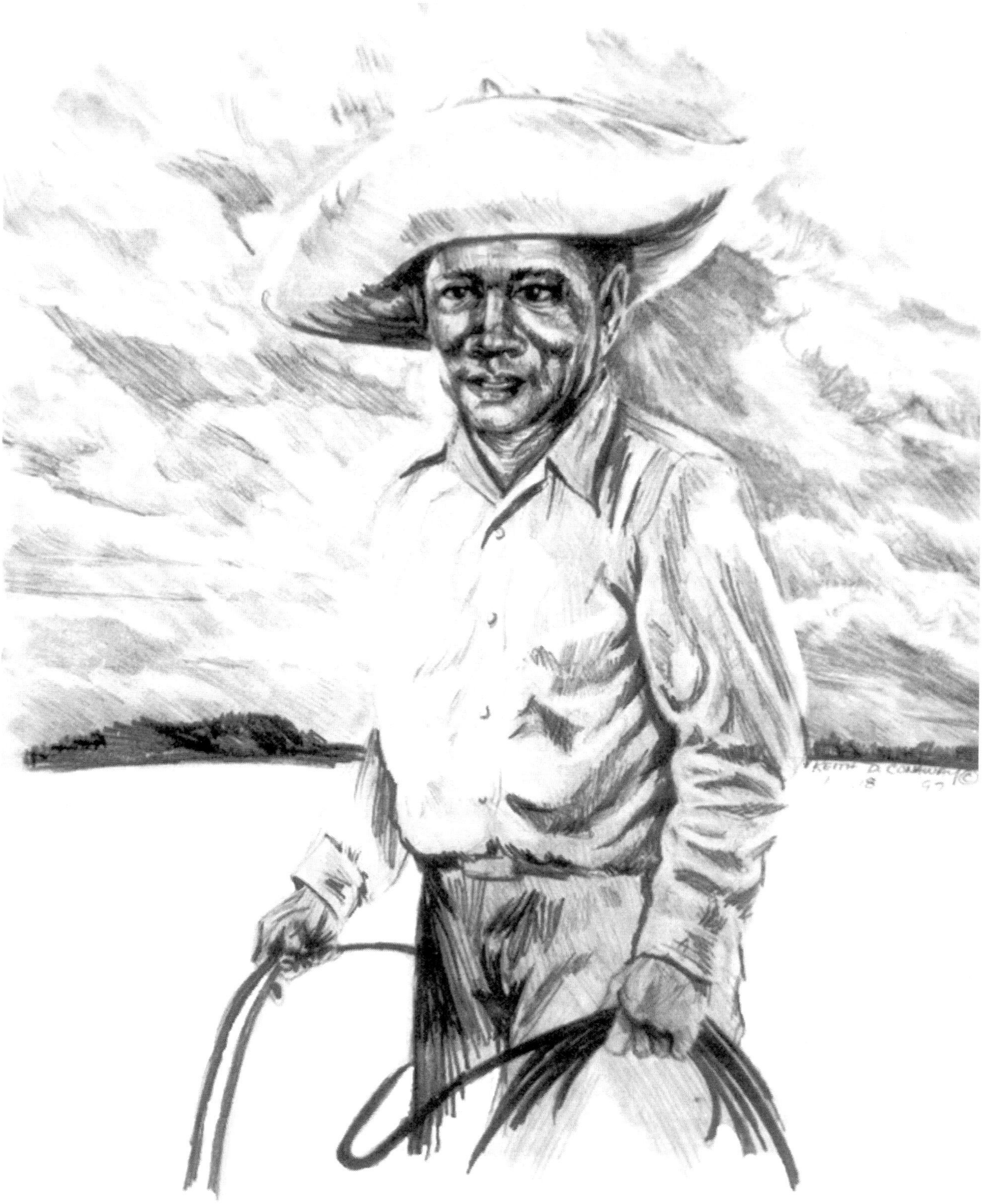

Bose Ikard: From Slave to Trail Drive Banker

Bose Ikard came to Texas from Mississippi when he was five years old as a slave of the family of Charles Goodnight. In adulthood he rode the Goodnight-Loving trail for four years as Goodnight's banker on cattle drives because no outlaw would believe that a black man would be carrying large amounts of money. Sometimes he would carry as much as $20,000 in cash, the proceeds from the cattle drive. Always during the drive, he carried the operating expenses of several thousand dollars for Goodnight.

In 1889, when he was forty-two, he returned from one last drive and planned to homestead in Colorado. Goodnight, his friend and counselor, persuaded him to buy a farm in Texas so they could stay in close touch. Upon Ikard's death in 1929 at the age of eighty-three, Goodnight wrote his epitaph:

Bose Ikard

Served with me four years on the Goodnight-Loving Trail, never shirked a duty or disobeyed an order, rode with me in many stampedes, participated in three engagements with Comanches, splendid behavior.

Goodnight just did not have room to record all the accomplishments of Ikard on his tombstone. He was probably the greatest drover that ever lived. He was a cook, an unequaled nighthawk [a night herder], a wrangler and bronc buster. As Goodnight told James Haley, "surpassed any man I had in endurance and stamina."

Certainly his stamina was amazing. When Goodnight, who had more stamina than most men on the trail, could no longer ride, he asked Ikard to take his place. "He never failed to answer me in the most cheerful and willing manner. He was the most skilled and the most trustworthy man I ever knew."

The Black West in Story and Song

Still there is a trace of racism in Goodnight's evaluation of Ikard when he said, "He paid no attention to women." On the Texas frontier there were few women, and still fewer black women. So to keep peace it was important that Ikard "paid no attention to women." In a male society, Ikard was a man's man.

Sometimes stampedes and Comanche raids were all in a day's drive, or in some cases, all in four days' work. On the second drive on the Goodnight-Loving Trail, Comanches had tried to capture the herd by stampeding them. For four days, Goodnight, Ikard, and the other drovers fought Indians and tried to round up the cattle.

On the fourth day, the cattle, shot up by Indians and nervous from storms, stampeded again toward the camp. Goodnight grabbed a blanket and jumped in front of the stampeding cattle to split the herd around the wagon and the bedrolls where his men had been sleeping seconds before.

Then at daylight he rode after the herd, wondering why Ikard who had been riding night herd hadn't turned them. Just as he almost caught up with him, Ikard saw him. In Goodnight's own words, "Immediately his horse shot out like lightning and he threw the leaders around."

As soon as the cattle were herded in a circle, Goodnight asked Ikard why he hadn't turned the stampeding cattle sooner. His answer showed his cheerful nature even after four days of stampedes and marauding Indians.

"'Well, I'll tell you sir,' he grinned, 'I wasn't certain who had the herd until I saw you. I thought maybe the Indians had 'em, and I sure wasn't going to help the damn Indians round up our cattle'" (Drotning 133).

Other African-Americans served in similar capacities on the trail drives. "Old Bat" was Texas John Slaughter's cook, but he could do almost any ranch work and served as a fiddler and fifer, valet, practical nurse, and bodyguard. When Slaughter went on cattle-buying trips, "Old Bat" always went along to protect the $10,000 in gold. In Mexico, when bandits tried to steal the silver Slaughter had for buying cattle, he and another black cowboy stood at Slaughter's side and helped turn back the attack.

Jim Kelly, known as Nigger Jim to his boss Print Olive and other cowboys and ranchers, was a wrangler, bronco buster, and gunman. When Olive went to Fort Kearney, Nebraska, in 1869, Kelly accompanied him and returned with

Cowboys, Ranchers, and Riders: *Bose Ikard*

him carrying saddlebags filled with currency and gold. In 1872, Kelly saved Olive's life when he had been wounded three times and was about to be killed.

Neptune Holmes, known as "Old Nep," served in a similar capacity for "Shanghai" Pierce. He accompanied Pierce on his cattle-buying trips for thirty-five years, leading a mule carrying the saddlebags filled with money. At night Holmes would use the saddlebags as a pillow to guard them.

As Porter has written, "Where large sums of money were involved, and courage and loyalty in protecting and defending it was needed, prominent cattlemen such as Goodnight, Slaughter, Olive and Pierce, characteristically preferred to depend on Negro bodyguards" (510).

Such was a rather strange set of affairs when black cowboys had to work harder and endure more than their white counterparts on most ranches and trail drives. They also met with discrimination and segregation on most ranches and drives. They frequently were assigned the most difficult jobs, sometimes attacked by unreconstructed southern cowboys, and usually paid less. Regularly, loyalty to the ranch overcame previous loyalties and prejudices. Necessity caused the black and white cowboys to work together and fight together.

Charles Siringo, in his autobiography, wrote that time and again black cowboys saved his life from mad steers, wild broncs, and even a hired assassin. There are many stories about treacherous river crosses with blacks saving whites and whites saving blacks from drowning.

Yet the legends of the Texas range still hold that Bose Ikard was the greatest top hand of all. He could cook, rope, and ride as no other man, and he was fearless enough to be a trail banker.

"Bois Ikard - All Around Cowhand"

(CHORUS)

Bois Ikard all around cowhand,
Rode out west with the best.
And forged himself a name.

Trail Banker, Bronco Buster,
Biscuit baking cowboy.
One of the best in the west,
and filled with Texas pride.
Learned real soon to get it right,
Pretty good with a forty-five.

Four years he rode, on the
Goodnight-Loving trail,
Those nights were seldom good my friend,
and hardly a loving trail.
Always the threat of death and danger
lurking at your tail.
Storms, stampedes and rattle snakes,
Sometimes midnight raids.
100 ways to hurt and die
and a life to try and save.

(CHORUS)

Hard work and violence,
Sometimes to survive.
Driving Texas long horns many
times was a do or die.
Eighteen hours in the saddle,
riding sun to sun.
Pushing self to the limit,
and sometimes beyond.

(CHORUS)

He lived to be <u>Eighty</u> <u>Three</u>,
and earned his bragging rights.
From Oliver Loving and none other
than "the one and only," Charles Goodnight.

Bois Ikard
Trail Banker

Words and Music by:
 Cecil Williams

Bois I-kard, all a-round cow-boy, rode out West with the best and forged him-self a name.

Verses:

Trail bank-er, Bron-co bust-er, Bis-cuit ba-kin' cow-boy. One of the best in the West, and filled with Tex-as pride. Learned real soon to get it right, pret-ty good with a for-ty five.

Copyright   Rolla, MO.

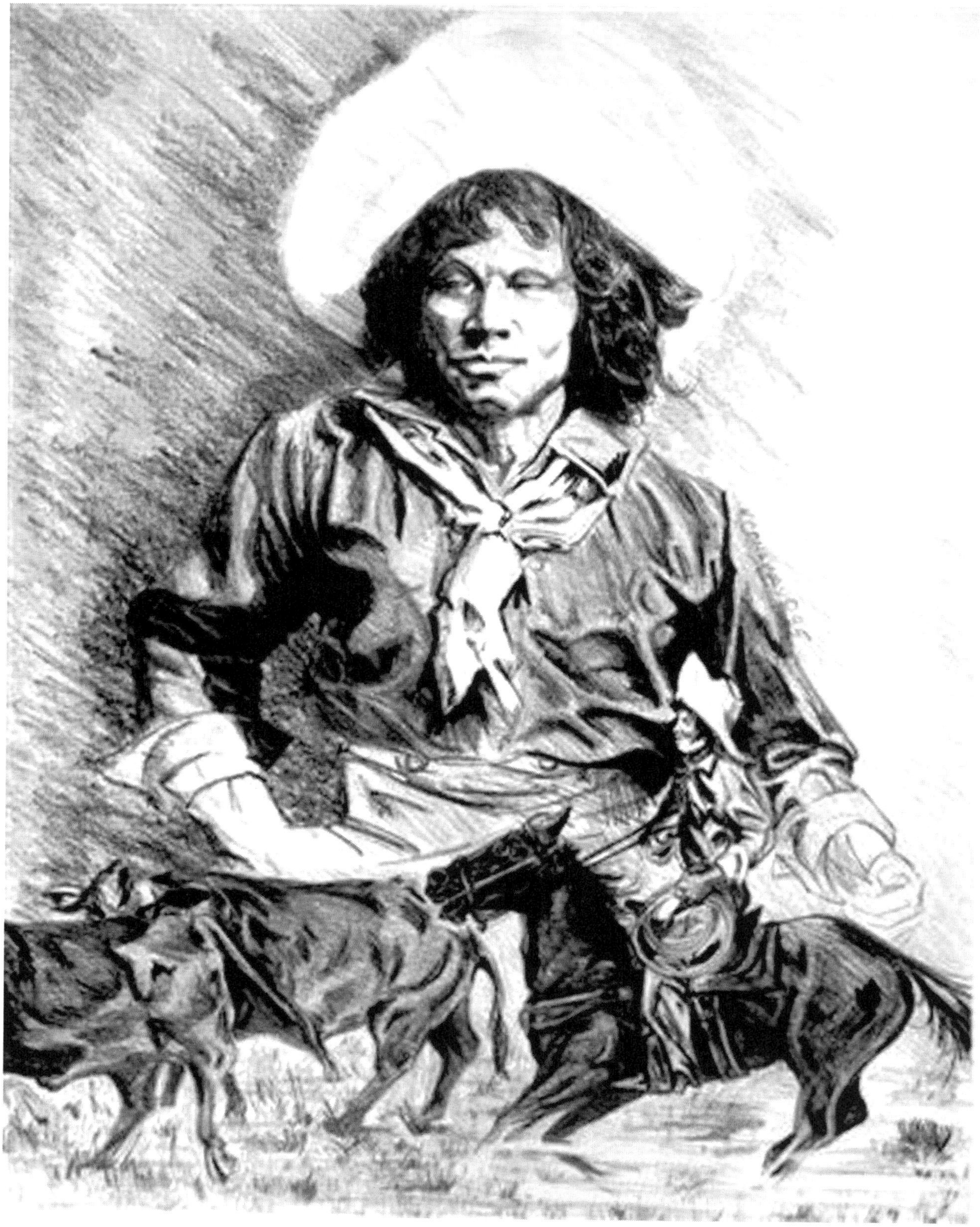

Nat Love, Deadwood Dick

Nat Love's journey from Tennessee slave to western cowboy to Pullman porter spans the history of modern America. He lived through the calamity of slavery to become a worker in modern technology. For a man who experienced adventures with Indians, outlaws, cowmen, it must have seemed claustrophobic to leave the freedom of the open range for the confines of a sleeping car.

Such was the life of a man who became known throughout the West, first as Red River Dick, and then Deadwood Dick. He broke horses with the best, and he counted as his friends Bat Masterson, Frank and Jesse James, Billy the Kid and Pat Garrett. He became the first cowboy hero of pulp fiction.

Although he ostensibly left his home in Tennessee in 1869 because of the lack of educational opportunities, the openness and freedom of the West left him little time for formal education. He quickly learned his trade as cowhand earning thirty dollars a month shortly after he arrived in Kansas. He relished the outdoor life that had few color barriers on the trail drives from Texas to Dodge, Abilene, and other cow towns.

Love was more than a cowboy adventurer, though. In his autobiography, he always displays a social awareness and conscience. In recalling "slavery days," he writes, "Go and see the play of 'Uncle Tom's Cabin,' and you will see the black man's life as I saw it when a child. And Harriet Beecher Stowe, the black man's Savior, well deserves the sacred shrine she holds, along with the great Lincoln, in the black man's heart" (13).

Katz regrets Love's "typical western braggadocio" and his failure to give more details about life on the trail. Still he was very much a part of the tall tale tradition of the West and retained his sense of humor even while boasting. "I gloried in the danger, and the wild and free life of the plains, the new country I was continually traversing, and the many new scenes and incidents continually arising in the life of the rough rider" (45). He brags about his ability to use a 45 colt, but modestly observes, "I became fairly proficient and able in most cases to hit a barn door providing the door was too far away" (45).

Still we have to wonder if any one could have had all the adventures he claimed to have had, be in all the gun fights he claimed to have been in, known all the famous outlaws he said he knew and survive to take such a conventional job as a Pullman porter. According to Love, early in his career he learned Spanish from the Mexican drovers, became a chief brand reader, and the top bronco buster and steer roper of the outfit. In every trail town he enjoyed the pleasures of women and liquor equally with the white riders.

Unlike 80 John Wallace or Bose Ikard, Love was not a black man who passed up his pleasures to save money to buy his own spread. He seems to have no ambitions in that direction at all. Perhaps he felt that owning his own ranch would have taken away the freedom of the wandering life.

His wanderings took him to the Powder River Country of Northern Wyoming on a trail drive where he faced the dangers of Indians demanding a toll, the ensuing fight, and a later buffalo stampede resulting in the death of a rider. He took all of these adventures with his usual aplomb, commenting, "But we did not get discouraged, but only wondered what would happen next. We did not care much for ourselves, as we were always ready and in most cases anxious for a brush with the Indians, or for the other dangers of a trail, as they only went to relieve the dull monotony of life behind the herd" (63).

If discovering new cattle trails in Arizona and Utah were not enough to make him a hero among cattlemen, his next drive took him into the Hole-in-the-Wall country where he had a "little shooting scrape."

> *Then as now this hole in the wall country was the refuge of the train robbers, cattle thieves and bandits of the western country, and when we arrived the place was usually full of them, and it was not long before trouble was brewing between our men and the natives which culminated in one of our men shooting and killing one of the bad men of the hole. (69)*

Because they had responsibility for 500 head, Love's outfit left quickly to avoid more shooting.

But his cool boastfulness is balanced by his sense of humor and his ability to laugh at himself. On a buffalo hunt, he impetuously decided to lasso a bull

Cowboys, Ranchers, and Riders: Nat Love, Deadwood Dick

with the results that he lost his lariat, saddle and horse, and nearly broke his neck. An incident quite similar to this is found in Twain's *Roughing It*.

On another occasion he rode into Mexican saloon on horseback and ordered a drink for himself and his horse. He seems to have assumed many white attitudes at this time because he refers to the Mexicans as greasers. Still he shows his social conscience in his incident. "I hated to have to hurt some of them but I could see I would have to or be taken myself, and perhaps strung up to ornament a telegraph pole." Riding out of the saloon firing his guns, he escaped.

Later adventures led him to be wounded seriously in an Indian fight, captured, and nursed back to health by Yellow Dog's tribe. Here after fighting the Indians for years rather than paying various tribes tolls on cattle drives, Love gained a respect for them and their medicine, which quickly healed his wounds. "My nose had been nearly cut off, also one of my fingers had been nearly cut off." This was the result of the hand-to-hand fighting with the Indians after he had run out of ammunition and already been wounded in the chest and leg.

Perhaps because of his bravery or perhaps because Yellow Dog's tribe was composed of "large percentage of colored blood," he was made a member of the tribe and betrothed to a beautiful squaw. To avoid this marriage, he made his escape and rode 100 miles bareback to safety.

Even this close brush with death and marriage did not dampen Love's rambunctious nature. After recovering from his wounds, he rode on the next drive to Dodge City where bad whisky made him rope a United States Army cannon at Fort Dodge to take back to Texas for Indian fighting.

Fortunately, his old friend, the town marshal, Bat Masterson, saw the humor in his canon stealing and fined him a round of drinks for the house, including his army captors. That fine came to fifteen dollars, but Masterson enjoyed the joke so much that he paid for the round, telling Love that he was the only cowboy he had ever liked.

On a drive to Lincoln County, New Mexico, during that range war, he met Billy the Kid and Pat Garrett. Love thought of the Kid as a cowboy who had been cheated in a cattle rustling scheme by John Chisolm, causing him to go on a rampage killing Chisolm's men. Love did recognize Billy as a dangerous killer who had murdered at least one man for each of the twenty-two years he lived before Pat Garrett killed him. Of Garrett, Love wrote he was "...one of the nerviest men of that country of nervy men..." (121). He also wrote of Garrett, "...behind the pleasant twinkle in his eye and the warm hand clasp there is a head as cool and a nerve as steady as ever held a 45" (122).

Throughout his career as a cowhand, Love had enjoyed the liquor, gambling, and women of the trail towns. In Mexico he fell in love for the first time in his life. She was a Mexican woman, whose mother would not want her to marry a "wild cowboy." Nevertheless, after a separation of six or seven months, they were re-united upon Love's next drive to Mexico. They became engaged but before they could marry, she died. That experience caused him to become even a wilder cowboy. "Her death broke me all up and after I buried her I became very wild and reckless, not caring what happened to me and when you saw me in the saddle you saw me at home, and while I saw many women since I could never care for any as I did for her" (127).

Now civilization was fast encroaching on the range. By 1889, Love left the life of trail driving to marry and become a Pullman porter. Of his wife, he wrote, "...she is with me now a true and faithful partner, and says she is not one bit jealous of my first love, who lies buried in the city of Old Mexico" (130).

Despite entering a more sedate, conventional occupation, Love did not forget his companions on the Great Plains. In writing his autobiography in 1907, he recalled knowing Buffalo Bill, the James brothers, Kit Carson, Yellowstone Kelly in addition to Bat Masterson, Billy the Kid, and Pat Garrett. Of Buffalo Bill he wrote,

> *It was a pleasure to meet often during the early seventies the man who is now famous in the old world and the new world, Buffalo Bill (William F. Cody), cowboy, ranger, hunter, scout, and showman, a man who carried his life in his hands day and night in the wild country where duty called, and has often bluffed the grim reaper Death to a standstill, and is living now, hale, hearty, and famous. (156)*

He remembers the James brothers as true men who took from the rich and gave to the poor just as the ballads say. Usually he is quite neutral politically,

Cowboys, Ranchers, and Riders: Nat Love, Deadwood Dick

but in comparing the James boys' ethics to the ethics of the rich he becomes something of a socialist, in writing,

> *The James brothers stole from the rich and gave to the poor, while these respected members of society [the wealthy] steal from the poor to make the rich richer, and which of them think you reader, will get the benefit of the judgment when the final day arrives and all men appear before the great while throne in final judgment? (157)*

He said of Kit Carson, Yellowstone Kelly, and the other scouts, hunters, and trappers he had known, "...they can all be described in one sentence, they were men whom it was a pleasure and honor to know" (157).

Katz is skeptical about how many famous westerners Love actually did know and how many of the daring adventures involving life and death he actually participated in. Perhaps he is right in thinking that Love seems to have forgotten he was black as soon as he went west. Certainly, he seems to have been uncritical in his judgment of outlaws, cowboys, mountain men, soldiers, and lawmen. He admired them all. Also he seems to have suffered more wounds than any one could possibly survive.

While we must grant that he exaggerated his exploits, we much also recognize that he did not brag and boast more than most westerners of that time including Buffalo Bill and the James brothers. Both the showman's and the outlaws' careers were based on shrewd publicity. At least, Love in his autobiography does claim that "every event chronicled in his history is based on facts." While he does write he has tried "to record events simply as they are," he does not make an absolute claim to truth. (Preface)

What he does show in his autobiography, in addition to his boastfulness, is sensitivity to his fellow frontiersmen and an awareness of the social changes that have taken place in America. In his Preface he remembers, "the playmates of my boyhood," "the few friends, who assisted myself and widowed mother," and most of all the comrades who rode with him. In his conclusion he recognizes the old way of life is gone.

> *Life today on the cattle range is almost another epoch. Laws have been enacted in New Mexico and Arizona which forbid all the old-*

time sports and the cowboy is almost a being of the past. But, I, Nat Love, now in my 54th year, hale hearty, and happy, will ever cherish a fond and loving feeling for the old days on the range, its exciting adventures, good horses, good and bad men, long venturesome rides, Indian fights, and last but foremost the friends I have made and friends I have gained. (162)

So the man who was born a slave and honored with the title Deadwood Dick after winning several events at the Deadwood City, Dakota Territory, Rodeo, embodies the progress of America from the frontier to modern technology. As an American, Love embraced the frontier and technology by being both "the wild and woolly cowboy" and the Pullman porter.

"Dead Wood Dick"
Nat Love

When the last song has been sung,
and the very last story has been told.
There is just one more little story, I feel
my friends ought to know.
Once there was A young bronco
buster, He came from Tennessee.
Just A plain 'ol Country Boy, And
the west he choose to see.

He rode into Dodge City, Kansas
A bustling frontier town.
Dance halls, Saloons and Pleasure
girls, He had never before been around.

There was drinking, Gambling and
fighting he had never before seen.
Everything was so rough raw and
wild, The young man was only fifteen!

(CHORUS)

Nat Love was a cowboy's cowboy!
He was one of a kind. And he
rode throughout the west, He
was a Hero of his time.

His first job was punching Texas
Long Horns, Thirty Bucks a month
was his pay. He rode from sunup
till sundown. He earned one dollar a day.

Many many years he did ride! The
Shawnee and Chisolm Trail, The
Good-Night Loving and The Western,
Sometimes that 'ol Santa Fe.

Sometimes he fought the hardest fight,
Sometimes he made the longest ride!
Fourteen time he'd been wounded,
Damned lucky he was to be alive!

Now the year was 1876, and
The fourth of July it was and
a wild west Rodeo Day.

There was riding and roping
Bronco Busting, Rifle and Pistol
shooting too.
There were Indians, Cowboys,
Pioneers and Gamblers, All
came to see what they could do.
The record said he won that
day, He beat the very best.
He was champion of the cowboys,
The best in the west.

The folk of Dead Wood City proclaimed
him Dead Wood Dick!
It's been over one hundred years
since he rode. Still they remember
him yet.
Nat Love was a Cowboy's Cowboy,
And was one of a kind.
Nat Love was Dead Wood Dick.
He was a hero of his time.

The Ballad of Deadwood Dick
Nat Love

Words and Music by:
Cecil Williams

When the last song has been sung: And the ve-ry last sto-ry has been told. There's just one more lit-tle sto-ry I feel that my friends ought to know. Once there was this young bron-co bust-er, He hailed from the state of Ten-nes-see. Just a plain ol' eve-ry day coun-try boy, And the West is where he chose to be.

Chorus:

Nat Love was a cow-boy's cow-boy, He was one of a kind. Nat love was Dead-wood Dick. He was the he-ro of his time.

to next verse:

Copyright November 5, 1976 East Palo Alto, CA.

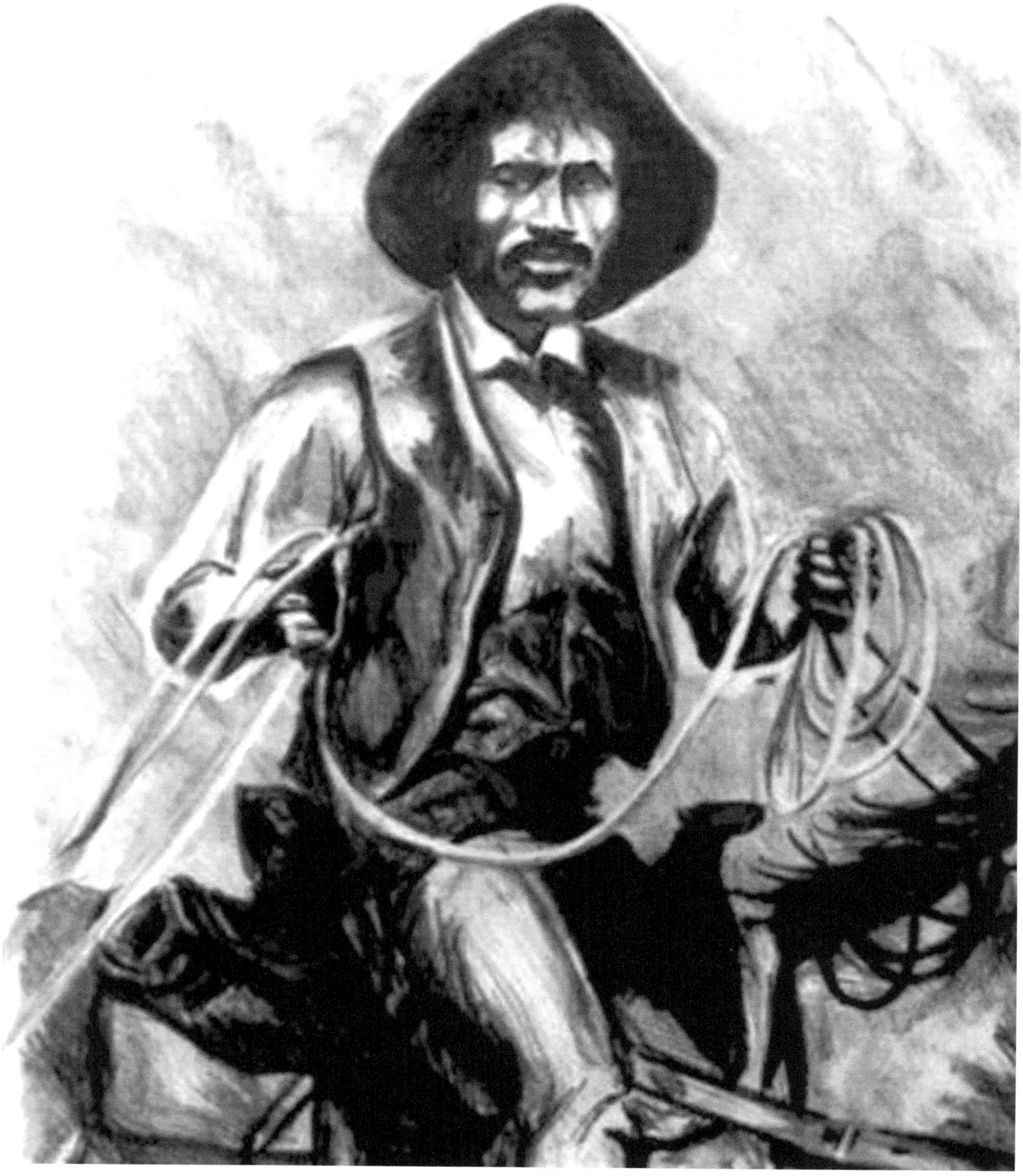

Isom Dart, the Black Fox

The code of the west required a cowboy to be a man of strength and stamina on the trail and a man of gentleness with women and children. Isom Dart was such a cowboy and such a gentle man.

Isom Dart's master had taken him further South during the Civil War to escape the invading Union army. During this time Dart served a group of Confederate officers as an orderly, cook, nurse, and scout.

Freed from slavery after the war, he drifted through Texas and Mexico trying all sorts of jobs, including being a rodeo clown in Mexico. While south of the border, he joined with a Mexican cowboy named Theresa to steal horses, swim them across the Rio Grande, and sell them in Texas. He gave up horse stealing to try mining in Colorado and working for a Chinese cook.

Tiring of these occupations, Dart turned to wild horse breaking and soon gained a reputation as the best horseman in the Green River country. John Rolfe Burroughs wrote, "...no man in the country understood horses better than Isom did." Dane Coolidge wrote that Dart "was considered the best bronco rider that ever threw a leg over a horse" (Durham 77).

But the gentle side of Dart was brought out by a Shoshone woman named Tickup and her nine-year-old daughter, Mincy. Tickup had run away from her brutal husband and found a home with Dart, who treated her with kindness and had a father's affection for Mincy. For Mincy, Dart was the only real father she had even known. But when her husband found them, Tickup fled with her daughter to her tribe in Idaho.

Dart then returned to his old occupation of horse stealing, joining the Tip Gault gang in Brown's Hole with his old Mexican partner, Theresa. When an attempted raid on a herd went wrong, the entire gang except Dart was killed. Dart was saved because of his gentle side. He was nursing an injured gang member, when the rest of the gang was raided by cattlemen at their home camp. With this close escape from death, he decided to go straight and signed on as a wrangler with the Middlesex Land and Cattle Company.

On a neighboring ranch, Elizabeth Bassett lived with five children and a sick husband. Dart, again being a gentle man, did what he could to help her, even taking her a steer when she needed food. The line between taking mavericks and rustling was a thin one on the Wyoming range then. To the large cattle ranchers, Dart was a rustler. The Hoy and the Scribner ranches had a warrant sworn out for him. Because of his reputation, no lawman would serve the warrant for some time.

Finally, Joe Philbrick, a deputy sheriff, agreed to bring Dart in for the reward. Philbrick rode to Brown's Hole, arrested him without difficulty, and was bringing him back to stand trial. As they traveled toward town, the buckboard he and Dart were traveling in turned over. The deputy sheriff was so seriously injured he could not move. Dart turned the buckboard right side up and caught and hitched the horses.

Instead of escaping, he transported Philbrick to Rock Springs where he put him in the hospital and turned himself in at the jail. He was tried for rustling, but his gracious, heroic act in saving Philbrick caused him to be acquitted. Philbrick testified for him at his trial.

Returning to Brown's Hole, he continued to be a favorite at the Bassett Ranch. When the Bassetts' daughter married Jim McKnight and they had two sons, Dart spent much of his time caring for them. He amused the children with songs and stories he remembered from his days as a slave on a plantation in Arkansas. He also did his rodeo clown act for them. Chuck McKnight told his mother, "Mama, I'll never have to go to a circus, 'cause I got a circus of my own" (Durham 80).

Because of his skill as a breaker of horses, and some say, because he was none too careful about the brands on stock, he built a ranch. He became one of the leaders of the small ranchers protective association along with Mrs. Bassett. Small ranchers in those days rounded up unbranded cattle before the round-ups of the big ranchers and stray calves less than a year old. Because the Wyoming cattle laws were written for the corporate ranchers, the small ranchers and nesters were violating the law in these practices.

The line between legitimate, small ranchers and rustlers became more and more blurred in Johnson County. From the standpoint of the big ranchers, Dart, Rash, and others crossed that line and became rustlers. The hired killer

Cowboys, Ranchers, and Riders: Isom Dart

of the Cattlemen's Association, Tom Horn, sent both Dart and Rash a written warning to leave Johnson County. When they didn't, an unknown assailant killed them both.

Rash was shot while he was sitting at his kitchen table eating breakfast. Even though he knew he was a marked man, Dart, at age fifty, thought he was too old to leave and start a new life. So he tried to surround himself with his friends for protection. Three months after Rash was killed, Dart walked out of his ranch house with two of his friends. A rifle bullet hit him in the back. While his friends ran for cover, the killer escaped without being seen. Common knowledge in the county held that Horn had killed both Rash and Dart.

Dart was buried on Cold Spring Mountain mourned by many good friends and the young Bassett boys, one of whom said, "I remember Isom as a very kind man. He used to 'baby-sit' me and my brother when Mother was away or busy." Other mourners recalled him as a "laughing sort of guy" and "a good man, always helpful." (Katz 158)

Today some people of Wyoming remember Isom Dart as a rustler. Others remember him as the best horseman they had ever seen even though he never entered a rodeo contest. Others remembered him as a faithful companion who protected and cared for women and children. Still others believe that Dart was a hero who died in a range war fighting for the rights of the individual against the corporate ranches. He was, ultimately, the westerner combining masculine strength with the gentleness of a natural gentleman.

"The Black Fox"

He was born a slave in Arkansas
Earned his nickname during the Civil War
He served with honor and he served with pride
But he never fought on either side.

He didn't start this dadgum war, so why should he fight?
If this be a brother's war, then, by God, let 'em fight.

(CHORUS)

The Rebels called him the Black Fox,
The Yankees called him crazy,
Well, maybe, but just like a fox.

It was out in West Texas they say he saved the day
Tracking a Commanche war party, making good their getaway.
Their captors he rode after, riding all alone,
and freeing the captives, brought 'em back, each and every one home.

(CHORUS)

A hero in this West Texas town, settlers said one of the best men around.
He tried real hard to ride that straight and narrow path,
But the trail was too crooked and his luck didn't last.
Riding west, he crossed the Rio Grande, south of the border he
met new friends (banditos amigos)
Northward he rode into Brown's Hole, joined Tip Gault and his gang.
Rounding up mavericks and branding strays, his days were numbered
from this day.

A hero, an outlaw, which was he?
In Texas a hero, Colorado a desperado, a good bad-man could he be?
A good bad-man was a dead man ol' Tom Horn said,
So a bullet in the back, the Black Fox was dead.
Now folk will always be a reckoning and a wondering why,
The Black Fox so loyal to ol' Johnny Reb and not the other guy.

(CHORUS)

The Black Fox
Isom Dart

Words and Music by:
Cecil Williams

Born a slave in Ar - kan - sas, earned his nick - name durin' Ci - vil War.

He served with ho - nor he served - with pride, Ne - ver fought on ei - ther side.

Chorus:

The Re - bels called him the Black Fox. Yan - kees called him cra - zy. Well, may - be but just like a fox.

to next verse:

Copyright November 7, 1988 Rolla, MO.

Keith D. Conaway © 2003

Ben Hodges

Scalawags and tall tales have always been a staple of America. Even better for American comedy are the scalawags who tell tall tales. From Rip Van Winkle to the Arkansas Traveler to V. K. Ratliff, Americans have saved a warm place in their hearts for storytellers on the outer edge of honesty. For the cattlemen of Dodge, Ben Hodges was their favorite--a scalawag and a storyteller.

Hodges arrived in Dodge City as a hand on a cattle drive, but he had greater ambitions. An unclaimed Spanish land grant attracted his attention as a way to leave the dust of the trail and become a substantial citizen of Dodge. Since his mother was Mexican, he laid claim to the land. To prove his claim he went back to Texas and returned shortly with proof. Some say he did not ride quite so far as Texas to find or create his "proof."

His fellow drovers, and then, because of his ability to talk, the townspeople of Dodge and complete strangers supported his claim. Then he convinced the president of the Dodge City National Bank of his importance. He began to borrow from the bank without security and without much reasonable possibility of paying them back. Next the railroads of Kansas were so convinced of his landed aristocratic background that they gave him a free pass.

Inevitably his behavior caught up with him. He was accused of forgery, rustling, and cheating at cards, but he could talk his way out of any scrape. He always carried a six-gun and a long rifle. He had himself photographed with a menacing scowl on his face. In that photograph he looks as if he is the fiercest gunfighter in that gun-fighting town of Dodge.

Hodges was too shrewd to engage in gunfights when talking could solve any problem. He acted as his own lawyer when he was indicted for cattle rustling.

What me, the descendant of old grandees of Spain, the owner of a land grant embracing millions of acres, the owner of gold mines and villages and towns situation on that grant of which I am sole owner, to steal a miserable lot of old cows. Why, the idea is absurd. No, gentlemen, I think too much of the race of men from which I sprang to disgrace their memory. (Katz 157)

Mark Twain's Duke and Dauphin would have been proud to make such a speech in bilking their neighbors. Hodges' neighbors knew him well, saw the humor and drama in his speech, and acquitted him despite the evidence to the contrary. He was just too entertaining to send to jail.

Certainly the hangers-on in the Dodge saloons would miss his tall tales and card playing too much if he was in jail. So he continued to gamble with Wyatt Earp and run a variety of con games. His acquaintance with Earp and his success in defending himself against charges of cattle rustling probably emboldened him enough to apply to the governor of Kansas for an appointment as livestock inspector.

In his application he indicated to the governor that he had always been a loyal Republican, although his saloon friends had never known him to take an interest in an election unless there was money in it. The idea of Hodges being cattle inspector was a little absurd. It would be, as one cattleman said, "like a wolf asking to guard the sheep pen." So the cattlemen prevented him from receiving the appointment. Still they enjoyed his company, played cards with him, and told stories about his latest escapades and schemes.

In 1929 both Earp and Hodges died of natural causes. Earp had a national reputation as a town-taming marshal, largely through the publicity efforts of Ned Buntline and other pulp writers. Hodges had only the gamblers and cattlemen of Dodge to tell his story. Still they knew him well. When they buried him in the Maple Grove Cemetery, they placed him near other cattlemen and cowboys. As one of the pallbearers humorously said, "We buried Ben there for good reason. We wanted him where they would keep a good eye on him" (Katz 157).

Hodges, who had lived by his wits and fast talk instead of a gun, is remembered as an entertaining scalawag who had to be watched even in death.

"Ben Hodges - Genteel Ben, The Gambler"

They called him a thief, he stole no man's gold.
They called him a con-man, the best in the land.
He rode up from Texas on a dusty cattle drive,
Liked what he saw, stuck around for a while.
Ben Hodges was a card shark, a gambler, a cowboy
He was what he was: the real McCoy.

(CHORUS)

So I'll ask you my friend, who's conning who?
Your answer my friend is up to you.

He gambled on life and bet on his fate.
Never took a dime from a common soul.
He was slick with cards, enough to grow old.

Now ol' Dodge City was a wild cowtown.
Goodmen, badmen gunned each other down.
Sometimes they fought just for fun.
Knife, bull whip, or even side-gun.

At the OK Corral, he was there,
And lost a trigger finger in that wild affair.
Wyatt Earp, Dock Holliday and Bat Masterson,
And Ben Hodges, a native son.

The shoot-out at the OK Corral:
The real thing and the real McCoy.
No tinsel town fakes,
Or Hollywood cowboys.

(CHORUS)

A thief, a con-man, the best in the land?
Tho' he never stole gold, or land, or a soul?

So I ask you my friend, who is conning who?
Your answer is up to you!

Genteel Ben, the Gambler
Ben Hodges

Words and Music by:
Cecil Williams

They called him a thief, he stole no man's gold. They called him a con-man, the best in the land. He rode up from Texas on a dusty cattle drive, liked what he saw, stuck around for a while. Ben Hodges was a card shark, a gambler, a cowboy. He was what he was -: the real McCoy

Chorus:
So I'll tell you my friend, who's con-nin' who? Your answer my friend is up to you.

to next verse:

Copyright   Rolla, MO.

116

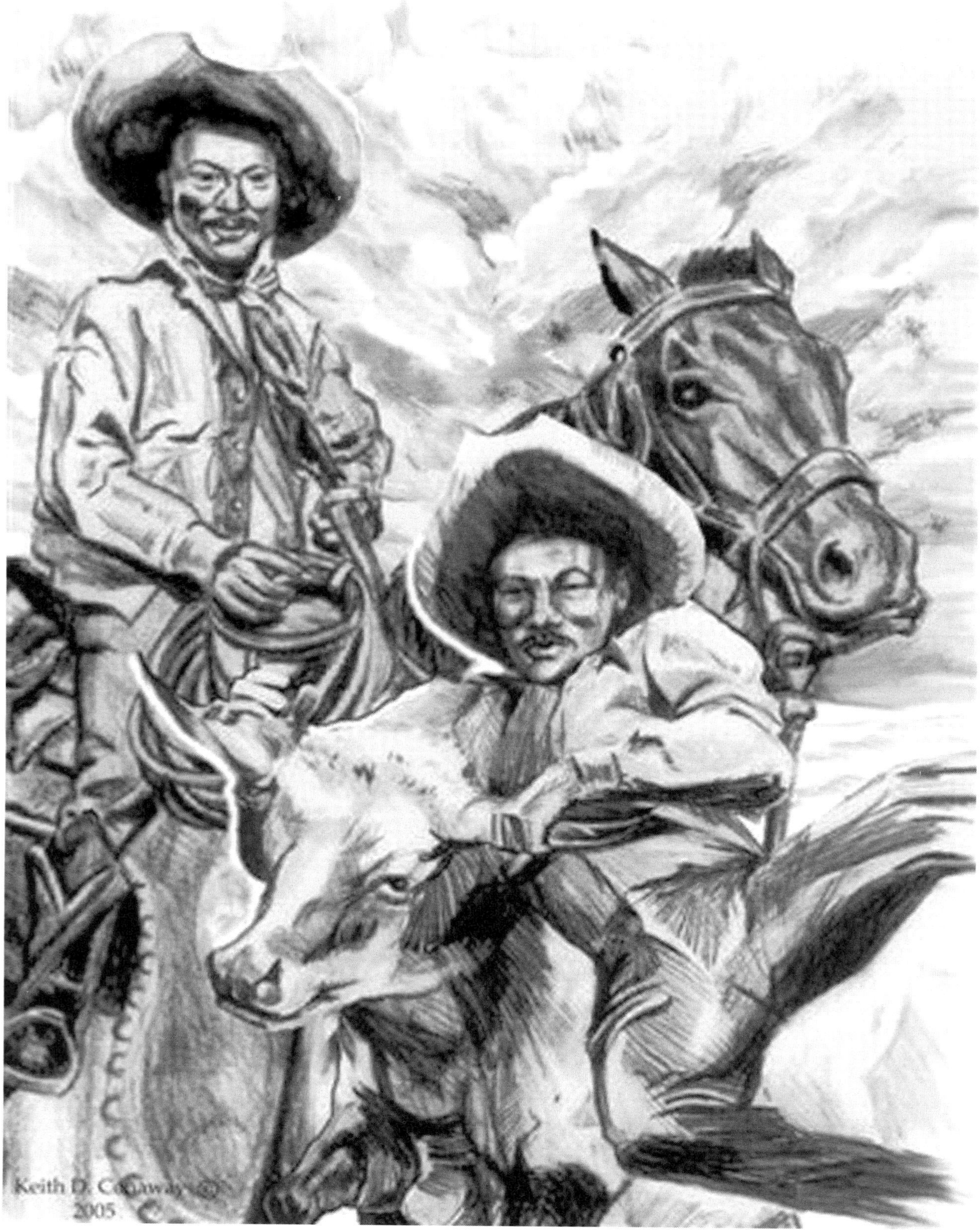
Keith D.
2005

Bill Pickett

Bill Pickett was the only rider whose name was listed in the program when the Miller Brothers 101 Ranch Rodeo performed in New York, Mexico City, and London, even though performers in the show included Will Rogers, Tom Mix, and other famous cowboys. He was the star of the rodeo because of his bulldogging act, which the program described as "The Wonderful Negro Pickett' Throwing Wild Steer by the Nose with His Teeth" (Durham 99).

He is often credited with inventing bulldogging. Probably it was a sport that was practiced before he became a rodeo rider. Durham credits a black cowboy named Andy, a top hand for cattleman Bill Hudson, with inventing it in an emergency when a longhorn steer escaped and he could not find his lariat. Another black cowboy who practiced the sport in the late nineteenth century was Sam Johnson in shows in Kansas.

But Pickett put his own brand on it. Fred Gipson described Pickett's style in the following way:

> *The way Bill went at it, he piled out of his saddle onto the head of a running steer, sometimes jumping five or six feet to tie on. He'd grab a horn in each hand and twist them till the steer's nose came up. Then he'd reach in and grab the steer's upper lip with his strong white teeth, throw up his hands to show he wasn't holding any more, and fall to one side of the steer, dragging along beside him till the animal went down. (Durham 97)*

Pickett joined the 101 Ranch at the end of the nineteenth century when he was about thirty years old. He had been born in 1870 to a Black Cherokee family in Oklahoma. His black ancestors had come with the Cherokee to Oklahoma on the Trail of Tears.

Before joining the Miller ranch, he had worked as a cowboy since he was ten. Early in his work, he developed the technique of holding calves quiet during branding that eventually evolved into bulldogging. He had also used the technique in the Texas brush country where a lasso was ineffective.

When he became a 101 hand, the ranch covered over 100,000 acres and employed 200 men, including many of the best cowboys to be found such as George Hooker, a black trick rider who could perform any stunt on a horse. Will Rogers later became a hand on the ranch.

In February, 1905, J. L. Gue, the promoter of the annual horse fair in Madison Square Garden, was looking for a gimmick to turn his losses into a profit. Zack Miller persuaded him that the 101 Ranch could do just that for him. Although other rodeos had not played well in New York, the rough and ready show of the Millers played to full houses in Madison Square Garden after its first show.

On opening night, during Pickett's bulldogging, the steer headed into the seats with people scattering and screaming. Pickett and Will Rogers were in hot pursuit, riding their horses into the stands. Pickett bulldogged the steer to the ground right there in the crowd. Rogers lassoed the steer's back legs and dragged it back into the arena with the black bulldogger hanging on. The crowd loved it.

There were no more steers stampeding through the grandstand for the rest of the run of the rodeo. The crowds filled Madison Square Garden every night although the seats where the steer had entered the first night were usually empty. Most people assumed that the steer went into the crowd because of stage fright. It was such a great publicity, it just might have been staged. Now the crowds came to see Pickett bring down the steers with his teeth while Rogers amazed them with his rope and Tom Mix showed his skills as a horseman.

For Rogers and Mix, the New York show was their first national recognition. Rogers went on to perform with the Zeigfeld Follies and become a national treasure as a movie actor, writer, humorist, and political commentator. Mix became one of the most famous cowboy movie stars in such films as "The Trouble Shooter," "Riders of the Purple Sage," and "The Last Trail." Later both Mix and Rogers had their own nationally broadcast radio shows.

Cowboys, Ranchers, and Riders: Bill Pickett

Pickett continued riding with the 101, although he acted in at least two silent movies, now lost. One is "The Bull-Dogger," and the other is a black cowhand mystery.

The next big rodeo the 101 Ranch staged for the National Editors' Association in the summer of 1905. It attracted 64,000 people. The thirty-five special trains the railroads ran could not carry all of the people who wanted to see the rodeo. The show was so good that the editors gave it publicity all over the country. For the next several years, the Miller brothers booked shows throughout the United States and in Mexico and Europe.

Pickett's greatest feat in bulldogging took place in Mexico City in 1908. The Miller brothers had angered most Mexicans by claiming "Bill Pickett's bulldogging act was a greater show than any Mexican bullfight." One of the brothers further irritated them by saying that Pickett could throw two steers in the time it would take a bullfighter to throw one.

This led to the bet that almost cost Pickett his life and Millers their rodeo. They bet that he could hold on to a fighting bull for five minutes. Bill well knew that he might be killed. The night before the match he asked Zack Miller, if he were killed, to bury him on the 101 Ranch in hard ground so the coyotes could not "scratch out his bones" (Mundis 54).

The betting between the Americans and the Mexicans became quite heavy. The day of the rodeo the capacity crowd of 25,000 filled El Toreo, the new steel and concrete bull-ring. The Millers had planned to stage the entire rodeo before Bill bulldogged the bull. The over-flowing, raucous crowd was not willing to wait for Pickett to throw the bull, or more likely, be killed. The Millers decided to stage the contest between Bill and the bull first.

His horse, Spradley, would not work close to the bull as it had always done with steers. When the bull gored the horse, Pickett slid off and grabbed the bull by the horns. Fred Gipson described what happened then.

> *For the next two minutes, the bull made a whipcracker out of Bill Pickett. He slammed the Negro's body against the arena wall. He threw up his head to sling the clinging man creature right and left, trying to dislodge him. He whipped him against another wall. He reached with his forefeet and tried to pry him loose. Finally he got*

The Black West in Story and Song

> *down on his knees and drove his sharp horns into the ground, time and again, trying to run Bill through. (Durham 101)*

Eventually the bull began to wear out, and after six minutes, when it was clear the timer was not going to ring the bell, the 101 riders roped the bull.

Pickett, bruised and battered, had won the bet. If he had lost, the Millers probably would have forfeited their rodeo because of the amount of money involved. Some say the Millers bet $10,000. Others say the original bet was $38,000 with Zack Miller raising it $10,000. The crowd was very large, estimated at 200,000. Pickett certainly earned his nickname, the Dusky Demon, that day.

For Zack Miller, he was "...the greatest sweat and dirt cowboy that ever lived, bar none" (*Black Indians* 184). Few would dispute Miller's claim. He was five foot six, 145 pounds, with the strength of a cowboy and the agility of a ballet dancer. His international fame was such that when the 101 Ranch went to London, he was introduced to the King and Queen and had dinner with an earl.

His popularity and skill attracted capacity crowds in London. When World War I broke out in 1914, the rodeo stock was seized to support the war effort. Pickett and the other rodeo performers returned to the United States. After the war, the Millers began presenting their show again. It was never as good as the one before the war, perhaps because Pickett was now between fifty and sixty years old.

He continued to work at the 101 Ranch every day. He also had his own spread of 160 acres to support his wife and nine children. In 1932, Zack Miller was the only Miller brother still living, but he was bankrupt, frail, and ill. Pickett, the last of the 101 rodeo riders, acted as his companion and nurse.

One day, Miller asked him to cut some horses for him. Pickett went into the corral on foot. One of the horses reared and struck him in the head with his hoof, knocking him down. The horse then stomped and kicked him as he lay on the ground. He died eleven days later. Zack Miller buried him on a high hill in hard ground on the 101 Ranch as Bill had requested in Mexico City twenty-four years before. In his memory Miller wrote a poem.

Cowboys, Ranchers, and Riders: Bill Pickett

Old Bill has died and gone away, over the Great Divide.
Gone to a place where the preachers say both saint and
sinner will abide.
If they "check his brand" like I think they will it's a runn' hoss
They'll give to Bill
And some good wild steers till he gets his fill.
And a great big crowd for him to thrill. (Durham 102)

From his home in Beverly Hills, California, Will Rogers recalled his old saddle pal in a letter to the New York *Times* dated April 15 and published April 16, 1932.

A little, small, good natured, likable negro died last week in Oklahoma, named Bill Pickett. Don't mean a thing to you, does it? Well, he was the originator of a stunt that has thrilled millions. It was the rodeo stunt of "bull-dogging."

When they arrest a cowboy for cruelty to animals in bulldogging, they arrest the wrong participant. More men get hurt than steers. He worked with white cowboys all his life and never had an argument or an enemy. Even the steers wouldn't hurt old Bill. (17)

Bill Pickett had made a good living as a rodeo performer and became a ranch owner. He never achieved the national and international fame and fortune that Will Rogers and Tom Mix did. He was elected to the Cowboy Hall of Fame in Oklahoma City after his death--the first black cowboy to receive that honor.

"The Legend of Dusky Demon"

Now gather folks lend a bending ear,
I'll tell you a story you really must hear.
I'll tell you a tale of a Black Cowboy and how he won his fame.
Bulldogging was his business, Bill Pickett was his name.
Bill Rodeod in the forty-eight states, and traveled the world around.
People came from many a mile to watch him dog 'em down.

Bill made legend many, many, year ago, South of
the Border in Old Mexico.
A Challenge was heard, a bet was made.
This is what happened, Now I'll tell you what was said:

Talk: Senior Col. Now we've been told there is a Dusky
Demon whose Tough and Bold.
Now we've got thirty-eight thousand, that says
he cain't throw and hold one of the meaniest
bulls in Old Mexico.
The Old Col. stratched his head and rubbed his
chin, looking at Bill, and he at him.
Then he winked his eye and slowly grinned.
Then he said "Boys" I'll cover that bet and will
raise it ten.
The bet was set the stakes were high.
The feat was for the fourth day of the month of July.

Over 200,000 stood silently by,
Surely this day 'This' Dusky Demon will die.
Trumpets had sounded, they played no more.
Impatiently waiting for Bill and el Torro.
Thundering of hoves were heard, louder and louder
they grew.
Then a warhoop cry and a rebel yell; leaping
from the saddle that Dusky Demon flew.
Bill grabbed those horns with a grip of steel.
Hold him he must and throw him he will, with a
mighty twist of Bill's strong hands.
El Torro's neck slowly began to bend.
Bill lunged forward with a bulldog's grip and
clamped his teeth into that bulls upper lip.

Then he threw himself to the ground to let his
weight help slow El Torro down.
El Torro grew tired, staggered and fell.
Bill knew he had just lived through a living hell.

He stayed on bending knee
removed his hat for all to see.
He then struck a familiar pose, as he held El
Torro down by his nose.
He then struck a familiar pose, as he held El
Torro down by his nose.
The fight lasted 26 minutes all toll; 10 to
throw and 16 to hold.
Bill Picket lived up to his fame, 48,000 dollars he did claim.
And his epithet it read: 'He's the greatest
sweat and blood Cowboy that ever lived.'
And he rode on the famous 101.

Now folks if you are ever out Oklahoma City way;
just take the time if you will.
Just drive on out to Persimmon Hill.
There you will see his picture and also you
will see his name.

In that Oklahoma Cowboy Hall of Fame.
In that Oklahoma Cowboy Hall of Fame.

The Dusky Demon
Bill Pickett

Words and Music by:
Cecil Williams

Ga-ther 'round folks lend a bend-in' ear I'll tell you a sto-ry you real-ly must hear;

I'll tell you a tale of a black cow-boy and how he won his fame, Bull-dog-gin' was his busi-ness Bill Pic-kett was his name.

Bill made le-gend man-y, man-y years a-go, South of the bor-der in old Mex-i-co

A chall-lenge was heard and a bet was made

This is what hap-pened and I'll tell you what was said.

Chorus:

Thun-d'rin' of hooves were heard, loud-er and loud-er they grew.

war hoop cry Aieee! wild re-bel yell -! lea-pin' from that sad-dle the Dusk-y De-mon flew.

to next verse:

Copyright April 12, 1973 East Palo Alto, CA.

126

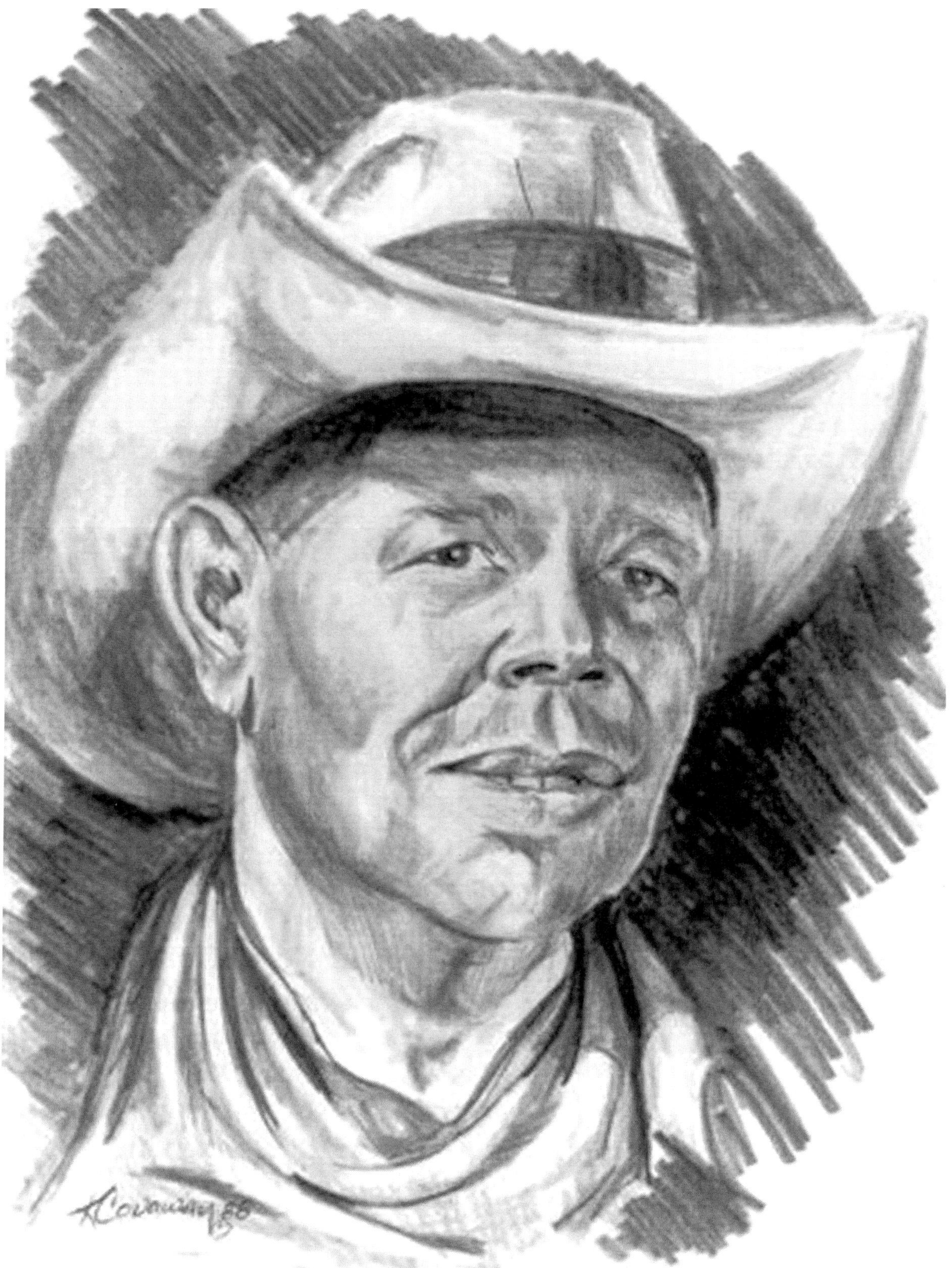

Nolle Smith

Westering is always moving forward toward the West. Nolle Smith was a westering man. In his early days in Hawaii, his good friend, Tony Soares said to him, gesturing to his heart, "Here, here inside, you'll always be a cowboy. What means paniolo? Not only fella rides horses, ropes cattle, but fella wants action, fella goes from one place to another, don't want stand still" (Gugliotta 83).

Certainly Nolle Smith never stood still or rested on his laurels. He was the son of a Scotch-Irish father and black-Indian mother. He worked as a cowboy on his father's Wyoming ranch and entered rodeos while still a boy. In high school he placed fourth in the wild horse race at the Cheyenne Frontier Days competing against professional rodeo riders.

He longed to go to West Point, but was twice rejected because of racial prejudice. Instead he went to the University of Nebraska where he was an outstanding athlete, especially in football, and an excellent student, majoring in mathematics and engineering.

After graduating from the University of Nebraska, he worked at a variety of engineering jobs in Denver. Then he decided to go to Hawaii. He took the opportunities Hawaii had to offer, first as a junior engineer for the Honolulu Public Works Department, and next as Superintendent of Docks of the Matson Navigation Company.

Soon he saw opportunities to start his own construction company and bring his entire family to Hawaii. His company was quite successful and he became well known on the islands. In 1928 a group of friends asked him to run for the Hawaiian Legislature as the representative from Kalihi. He campaigned in both English and Hawaiian becoming known as Kamika, the Hawaiian word for Smith.

In the legislature, his greatest work was done on the Education Committee to improve the quality of education for all Hawaiians regardless of race or creed. Because of his political responsibilities, he dissolved his construction business. He then served in various offices in the Hawaiian government.

During World War II he was Director of Civil Service for the islands. After the war he retired from territorial government at the age of sixty-five only to realize a life-long ambition.

He had from boyhood longed to serve his country, first as a West Point graduate and then as a diplomat. Those positions had been closed to him before World War II. In 1953, President Eisenhower appointed him Commissioner of Insular Affairs of the Government of the Virgin Islands. In that position, he took on the monumental task of trimming down the cumbersome bureaucracy of the territorial government. When Governor Alexander had to resign for reasons of health, the President offered him the governorship. He turned it down because as he told his wife, "we might be here the rest of our lives, and even with all its charm and tremendous advantages,...we want to see other places" (Gugliotta 153-54).

The westering spirit was still with him. The mayor of Quito, Ecuador, invited him to come there, to supervise the modernization of that city. He took that invitation because it was an opportunity to travel and practice the profession that he loved best, engineering. He did his work in Ecuador so well, that President Francois Duvalier of Haiti requested that the State Department send him to assist his government.

Throughout his life, Smith had been noted for his friendliness. The Ecuadorians said he had *amistad*, friendship, a friendly way of working with people. From the beginning he was in conflict with President Duvalier. Despite these conflicts, *Time* reported, "Nolle Smith, 70, a Negro economist from Wyoming, has helped cut petty corruption and inefficiency" (Gugliotta 171). Although he met with President Duvalier daily and his office was right across the hall from the President's, he could never establish a working relationship with him. Then he realized the reason for this when Duvalier made himself dictator of Haiti. Shortly after that, he left Haiti with his wife.

His next State Department assignment was in a place he had longed to go for many years--Brazil. There he was appointed Fiscal and Administrative Advisor for the Agency of International Development. He served in the capacity for five years when he decided to retire and return to Hawaii. He was now seventy-five and had served the State Department for ten years. Because of his outstanding service to his country, the State Department made him a contract

Cowboys, Ranchers, and Riders: Nolle Smith

consultant and cleared him to work for the United States government on a worldwide basis.

Now his westering days were over. He had gone from cowboy to engineer to legislator to diplomat. He enjoyed every one of his careers and had served his country well. He retired home to Hawaii to enjoy his final years with his wife, children, and grandchildren. Hiram Fong, an old friend and the first United States Senator from Hawaii, summarized Smith's life.

> *Nolle led a very active, successful life. To me his most notable feat was his election and re-election to the Territorial House of Representatives. He won a seat in the Hawaii Legislature from a district, which perhaps had no more than ten Negroes. The election proved how highly esteemed he was in the eyes of the non-Negro community. He was well liked and respected for his friendliness, his honesty, and his keen mind. (Gugliotta viii)*

"Nolle Smith"

He was born in a tent on Crow Creek Ranch
And he grew up on the land in ol' Cheyenne.
At Chugwater he learned to rope and ride.
On his Pinto named Absaroka that famous Indian tribe.

(CHORUS)

Paniolo! They called him, Hawaiian Buckaroo!
Paniolo! They called him, Hawaiian Buckaroo!

Nolle's family tree was truly a combination of
All that America is or at least ought to be.
His father was Scot-Irish, and once a scout for the Pony
soldier men.
And is mother was a proud Black Chocktaw Indian.

(CHORUS)

Now growing up on the mainland had it's up's and down's.
But life is just a challenge and solutions must be found.
So he set sail for Blue Hawaii and began a new career
With zest and Western spirit, the future held no fear.

He was a cowboy, an engineer, and a statesman traveling
throughout the land,
Doing his best to help his fellow man.

(CHORUS)

Virgin Islands to Hispaniola, working hard with ol' Poppa Doc
Trying once again to help put Haiti back on top.
He will always be remembered by his deeds and deeds alone,
Just a hard-working cowboy and Wyoming was his home.

(CHORUS)

Nolle Smith
The Hawaiian Buckaroo

Words and Music by:
 Cecil Williams

He was born in a tent on Crow Creek Ranch, and grew up on the land in old Chey-enne. At Chug-wa-ter he learned to rope and ride, And on his pin-to named Ab-sa-ro-sa, that fam-ous In-dian tribe.

Chorus:

Pan-i-o-la they called him, Ha-wai-ian Buck-a-roo -. Pan-i-o-la they called him -. Ha-wai-ian Buck-a-roo -.

to next verse:

Copyright May 20, 1988 Rolla, MO.

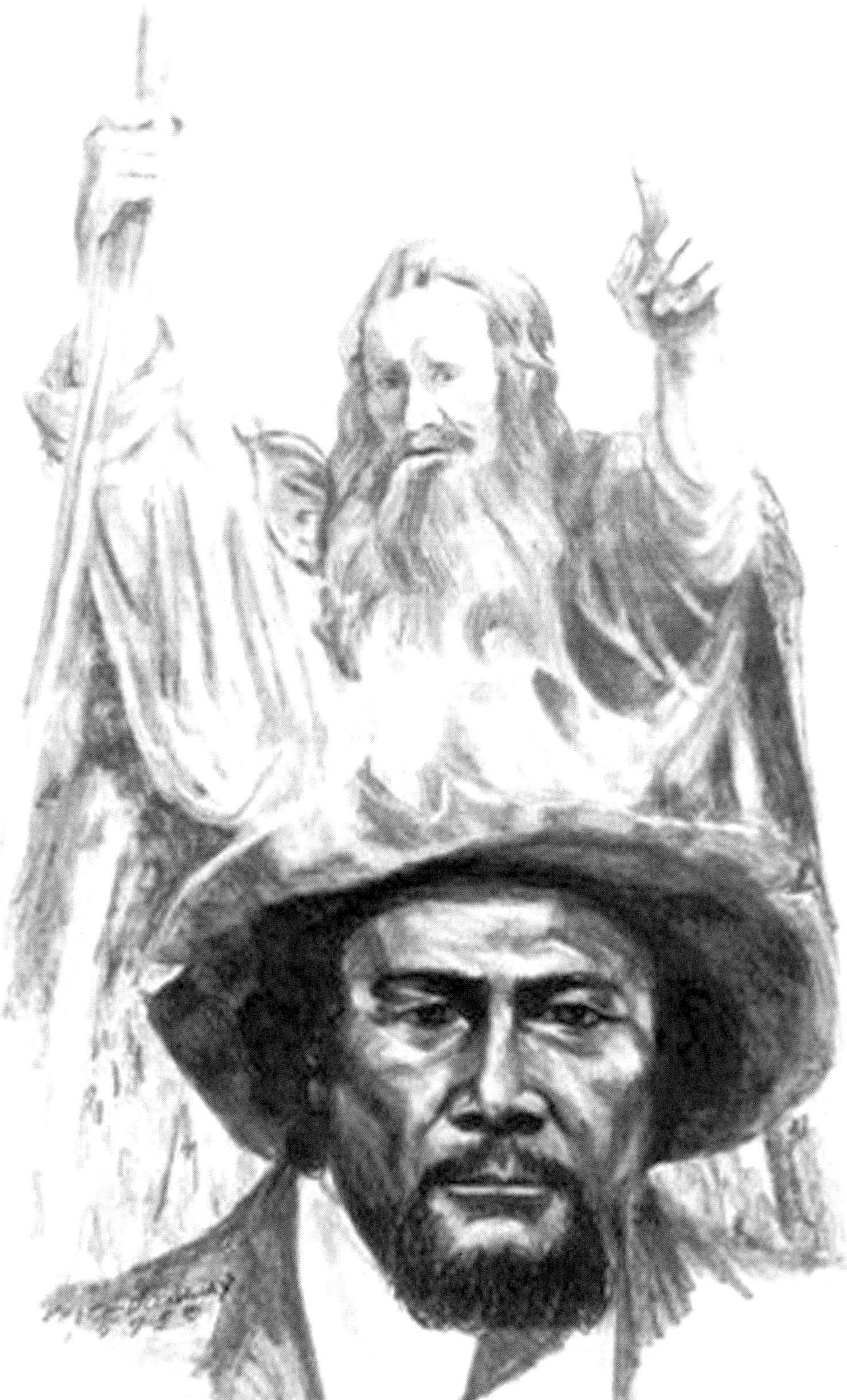

Town Founders, Townspeople, and Homesteaders

Benjamin "Pap" Singleton

To some Benjamin Singleton earned his nickname "Pap" because he was the black Moses he claimed to be. He had guided his people to the Promised Land of Kansas where they could be free landowners. For others Singleton was a shrewd real estate salesman. The reality is he was a bit of both.

The "Exodusters" as they called themselves made the Exodus from the Egypt of the South after the Civil War to the Promised Land of Kansas. This was the "Land of Milk and Honey" and freedom associated with idealism of John Brown. Singleton was not alone in encouraging black immigration west, but he was the most successful of the real estate promoters.

Singleton, as a slave in Tennessee, was sold by his master a dozen times or more into the deep South. Each time he would escape and made his way back to Tennessee and his old master. At last, tiring of being sold into the South, he escaped on the underground railroad to Windsor, Canada, after three failed attempts. For a time he followed his trade as a carpenter and cabinetmaker in Canada. Then, feeling a responsibility to others still in slavery, he crossed the river from Canada to Detroit to work on the underground railroad.

After the Civil War, he returned to Tennessee and was disappointed to find that the South had not changed all that much in regard to the rights of black people. Believing that former slaves must acquire land to have social and political freedom, he formed the Tennessee Real Estate and Homestead Association. Racial prejudice and expensive farmland in Tennessee doomed this enterprise.

Reluctantly, he gave up on Tennessee and decided that blacks would have to emigrate north to find the Promised Land. The development of the railroads in Kansas had opened up cheap land there, and Kansas had long seemed to be a land of freedom to southern blacks.

Naturally, most of the newly freed people had little money, but there were some who did. These were the people Singleton sought for his new colonies. He never encouraged any one to emigrate to Kansas unless they had money to pay for their transportation and buy land. He circulated, with the help of the railroads and steamship companies, chromos [an early form of colored photography] throughout the South depicting Kansas farms with black owners who had large, full barns, sleek animals, and ripe crops.

Because of other real estate promoters and rumors of free land, poor southern blacks rushed to Kansas. The promoters built clapboard barracks and raised money for food and clothing. Naturally, many white Kansans did not want the exodusters, especially the poor ones. The town of Atchison passed an ordinance prohibiting the "importation of paupers." Law enforcement officers of Leavenworth stopped a steamboat loaded with exodusters and refused to let them land. In Topeka white residents threw the lumber being used to build barracks for the emigrants in the river.

However, there were others who were quite generous in providing relief. The relief movement was nation wide. Churches and newspapers raised money as the Chicago Inter-Ocean urged to aid "the colored people who are fleeing from Southern oppression to homes upon our Western prairies" (Bontemps 64). John Deere, the agricultural equipment manufacturer, donated $100. Newspaperman Robert Ingersoll visited Kansas and was so impressed by the movement that he raised $1200 dollars from fellow businessmen. Aid came from England as well. The people of London sent $8,000, and perhaps more significantly, 50,000 pounds of food and clothing.

Soon Singleton recognized that mass migration of the poor would overwhelm the system of charity that had developed. So he urged only those who could afford to pay their passage and buy land to come to Kansas.

He started his first colony in Cherokee County, Kansas, in 1875. It was known as Baxter Springs or Cherokee Colony and had only three hundred settlers.

In his second venture, variously called Dunlap Colony or Singleton Colony, he started in 1878 in Morris County, southwest of Topeka. He had two black

Town Founders, Townspeople, and Homesteaders: *Benjamin "Pap" Singleton*

partners, A. D. Frantz and Columbus Johnson, and this colony had eight hundred settlers. The settlers bought government land for as little as $1.25 an acre, paying one-sixth down and the rest in six payments at six percent interest. Singleton and his partners received a commission on each sale. At that time, at least 80-180 acres of land was thought to be necessary to start a farm.

There were immediately various sources of friction with the white settlers of Morris County, including the refusal of whites to allow blacks to be buried in the white cemeteries. These conflicts were largely resolved by 1881. Eventually the colony was the education center for Kansas blacks. The Kansas Freedmen's Relief Association established the Literary and Business Academy there. Additionally, the colony had two elementary schools and a Quaker industrial school.

Singleton was the leading black advocate of colonies in Kansas, but there were other organizers and land speculators. Nicodemus was founded by a group of Topeka blacks in 1877 with the help of a white Indiana preacher, W.R. Hill. Hill had laid out the town of Hill City in 1876. He encouraged black emigration to the 100th meridian to increase the population and land values in the area even though it was not good farming land.

The town was named Nicodemus, not because of its biblical origins, but because the legendary slave who purchased his freedom. Blacks before the Civil War commemorated Nicodemus in rhyme and song:

Nicodemus was a slave of African birth
And he was bought for a bag full of gold;
He was reckoned a part of the sale of the earth,
But he died years ago, very old.

Hill claimed to be the founder of the colony. If he founded it, he apparently did so more for profit than for idealism. He did not intend for blacks to gain political power as he said: "We will have to make concessions to the niggers and give a few little offices, but when we get the county seat at Hill City they go to ____" (Athearn 76). His profits came from charging a locating fee of five dollars to each emigrant family, while paying only two dollars to the government to file for the land.

The "Exodus of 1879" was the height of the migration. One of the Exodusters told a Congressional committee, "The whole South--every state in the South--had got into the hands of the very men that held us as slaves. We said there was no hope for us and we better go" (Eyewitness 315).

Agreeing with the position that there was little chance for blacks to gain economic freedom in the South and seeing opportunities to promote his own real estate interests, Singleton continued to encourage emigration to black colonies he was instrumental in establishing. Because he felt that the former slave owners of the South could not change, he said, "[I] studied it all out, and it was cl'ar as day to me [that] my people couldn't live that. It was ag'n nature for the masters and the slave to jine hands and work together" (Athearn 288).

For him, political integration was not an immediate goal. In fact, he felt that blacks would benefit from segregation and would be harmed by integration. He believed that they should live free of white interference and manipulation in separate towns and communities. At first Singleton thought that Kansas was just the place. By 1879 though, he felt blacks were concentrating too much in Kansas. He urged them to spread out in the North and the West, where they could become landowners. In time too, he realized that separateness could not be maintained as transportation and communication improved.

By 1880 the migration had placed a drain on both skilled and unskilled labor in the South. Congress formed a committee chaired by Democratic Senator W. Voorhees of Indiana to investigate the situation. Voorhees and some other Democrats believed that the Republicans were encouraging emigration into Indiana and other northern states to gain political power. Many southerners felt that Singleton and other advocates of northern emigration were robbing the South economically.

Just before Singleton testified at the committee hearing, Henry Adams, a black union army veteran from Louisiana, gave his testimony. He gave the senators examples of the violence committed against blacks who tried to assert their rights in the South.

Singleton's testimony was less bitter than Adams and others who testified before him. Still he was quite firm in asserting that the black population was

Town Founders, Townspeople, and Homesteaders: Benjamin "Pap" Singleton

worse off under the new freedom than it had been during slavery. He was convinced that blacks must find freedom in the North by developing their own agriculture and industry, institutions and laws.

Vorhees kept pushing the idea that the emigration was a Republican plot. Finally, Singleton's mildness and natural friendliness reached their limits. He told the committee, "I am the whole cause of the migration. Nobody but me. I am the Moses of the colored exodus" (Bontemps 55).

He was overstating his role in the exodus, but he was not wrong in disagreeing with Vorhees. Blacks emigrated north during this period seeking freedom and land ownership. The emigration was not a Republican plot. Mozell Hill has argued, "As an alternative to the many colonization proposals for separation of the races, Negroes began voluntarily to isolate themselves in separate communities on the frontiers as a means of escaping white domination" (268).

Of course the harshness of the weather and the poverty of the land often proved too much for both black and white emigrants on the western frontier. Eventually, many who had come west with dreams of owning their own land gave up that dream. They emigrated to the cities of the North to work in the factories in the growing industrial revolution.

By 1881, Singleton, who was then seventy-three, recognized the movement was slowing down and the exclusively black communities were largely dying out. Blacks were scattering throughout Kansas and the United States seeking a higher standard of living.

Singleton continued to pursue his real estate interests and to remain socially and politically active. In 1882 the blacks of Topeka organized a picnic to honor him on his birthday. He invited every dignitary he could think of from the President of the United States down to the mayor. Few of these government officials attended. Some sent letters of regret, which Singleton gave to the newspapers. He always knew the value of publicity and how to turn a profit. The picnic cost each person five cents for admission, and he made fifty dollars profit. The next year the picnic had a profit of $274.25.

In the 1884 presidential campaign a rumor spread throughout the South that Cleveland would re-enslave the blacks if he were elected. This was enough for Singleton to search for a Promised Land outside the United States. He tried to raise money to make a trip to Cyprus to explore the prospects for black settlement there. That venture failed. In 1885 he organized the United Transatlantic Society to encourage immigration to Africa. His society never sent immigrants to Africa; however, it did put many applicants in touch with other immigration societies.

He also felt that industrialists and factory owners were lobbying in Congress for laws to encourage immigration to the United States from European and Asian countries. He felt Congress had written the new immigration laws to keep labor costs cheap and make employment for blacks harder to find.

In his last years, many thought of him as braggart who talked on and on about what he had done. He claimed to have settled 82,000 blacks in Kansas. No one knew how he arrived at that figure. Certainly, he exaggerated. Nevertheless, his dream had caused thousands upon thousands to emigrate north. When he died in Topeka at the age of eighty-three, newspapers throughout the nation reported truthfully in obituary notices that he was "The Moses of the colored exodus."

"Benjamin Pap Singleton (Black Moses)"

Emancipation war ended in 1865
And yet the plight of those freed dared to survive.
Mr. Lincoln signed our papers, "Now boys, I've set you free,"
"Now git to getting so you can be the best that you can be."

(CHORUS)

What about that forty acres on the day you set me free
And what about that dadgum mule, Uncle Abe, you promised me?

They were freed refugees and despised throughout the land
Up the creek, so to speak, in this God-fearing land
the bloody war was over, the fighting was done
But the flight to freedom, my friend, had just begun.

"Ship us back to Africa," Henry Adams did plea
"'Tis best for us to live and die in our own home country."
"Like holy hell!" ol' Pap yelled, half-cussin and a-cryin
"Brethren, we've paid our dues, and there's no denyin,"
"America is our home and where we ought to be,"
"So follow me, believe you me boys, I'll see you free."

(CHORUS)

That exodus of '79 was forty thousand strong
Forged their way throughout the South, looking for a home
Exodusters, sod-busters, people of the land
Fathers, mothers, sisters, brothers joined that rag-tagged band

He was a preacher, a teacher, a God-fearing man
With Winchester and Bible, he led that wagon train
Black Moses they called him, Benjamin was his name
Benjamin Pap Singleton led that wagon train

(CHORUS)

Good times a-coming, long, long time on the way
Nicodemus, Kansas those settlers made their way
Nicodemus, Kansas still around today.

Black Moses
Benjamin 'Pap' Singleton

Words and Music by:
Cecil Williams

E-man-ci-pa-tion war end-ed in eigh-teen six-ty five and yet the plight of those freed dared to sur-vive. Mis-ter Lin-coln signed our pa-pers, "Now boys I've set you free, now git to get-tin' so you can be the best that you can be."

Chorus:

What a-bout that for-ty a-cres on the day you set me free? What a-bout that dad-gum mule? Un-cle Abe, you pro-mised me.

to next verse:

Copyright February 5, 1990   Rolla, MO.

Keith D. Conaway © 2002

Mary Fields, Stagecoach Mary

Only two kinds of women existed in the West according to most men-- good women who were married or the fallen angel. Opportunities for women were quite limited on the frontier, although the region offered them more freedoms than the East. Riding sidesaddle was a social necessity in the East. Some women in the West escaped this social handicap working as cowhands and ranchers. A black woman was doubly handicapped in this male dominated society.

Mary Fields, also known as Stagecoach Mary, was not an angel and she certainly wasn't a creature for men to use. She took on most of the occupations closed to western women. She had been born a slave in Tennessee. She at one time or another was a stage driver, a saloon fighter, a gambler, a restaurant owner, a freight hauler, and the only woman authorized to carry the U. S. mail. She was always armed with a Winchester and a Colt revolver. She was ready to defend her rights with any male who tried to take them from her.

Even when working for a Catholic school for girls operated by Ursuline nuns, where she tended cows and chickens and hauled supplies, she was ready to defend herself. A male hired hand of the mission challenged her authority as a freight driver. She settled the matter by challenging him to a shoot-out. The bishop, not pleased that she had resorted to guns to settle an argument, dismissed her even though she was the only freight hauler known for delivering supplies in any kind of weather.

One snowy night when no one else dared haul freight, she did. The horses panicked when they heard the wolves howl. The wagon turned over spilling all the goods on the ground. She faced a long night, surrounded by wolves, with only her rifle as a companion. She survived that night and many other such adventures.

After the bishop fired her, Mary, six feet tall and powerfully built, was ready to take on other jobs. First, she tried something that many would consider more feminine by opening a restaurant. It failed because her heart was not in that kind of work. She loved the freedom of the plains too much.

The Black West in Story and Song

She returned to freight hauling and stagecoach driving. In her mid-sixties she won a contract for delivering the United States mail. She soon was famous for making her mail deliveries no matter what the weather or the terrain. Everyone now called her Stagecoach Mary.

When she was in her seventies, she took a more sedate occupation running a laundry in Cascade, Montana. Still she was known as a woman who would not allow any man to take advantage of her. One local tale is that she was in the saloon smoking cigars and drinking with her friends when she saw a man walk by who had refused to pay his laundry bill. She walked out on the street, knocked the man down with one blow, and returned to the saloon. There she told her friends, "The bill's settled."

Many Cascade residents remembered her as a hard drinking, bad-tempered woman who always carried a gun, and did other such unwomanly things such as frequent saloons, smoke cigars, and say exactly what she thought. Others saw a more feminine side to her and remembered her as soft-spoken, generous, and neighborly woman who grew flowers in her garden and attended all the town's baseball games.

When she died in 1914, most of the citizens of Cascade could not believe that the woman, Mary Fields, whom they knew as a citizen of their town, was the famous or infamous, Stagecoach Mary. She was buried in the Hillside Cemetery in Cascade with a simple wooden cross to mark her grave. But her influence was not so simple. Through her strength, courage, and sense of independence, she has set a high standard for the women of the West who have followed her, both black and white.

Mary Fields
"Stage Coach Mary"

Born in a cabin
In the mountains of Tennessee
The great Northwest,
Is where she longed to be.

She walked real proud,
and stood big tall.
Over two hundred pounds
and six feet tall.

Mary Fields, Mary Fields,
was a cigar smoking, whiskey drinking
gun toating, short tempered,
Female Tiger Cat.

(Only if you crossed her
otherwise) folks she was as
gentle as a kitten.
With a heart as pure as gold.

To a dying friend one day,
she made a vow.
I'll get the girls west,
someway, somehow.

With two young nuns,
she left one day.
Heading west,
Out Montana way.

The year was 1884
Those dauntless souls
were Westward Ho.

The record read,
The trek was made.
Her vow was kept,
Her debt was paid.

The frontier was raw,
It was wild.
You fought to survive,
Or you'd die.

Her hands were leather tough,
Her palms were calloused worn.
Hard work she'd always done,
Hard work she'd never shuned.

Loading freight, mail wagon
Mule skinner, laundry woman
and on the stage, she rode shot gun.

She had no fear of beast or man.
From a good fist fight, she never ran.

She was tough as a Tiger Cat.
And fit as a Grizzly Bear
Any way you chose to fight,
Any ole way was fair.

She had the spirit of a Eagle,
The heart of a mountain lion.
To no mortal man did,
Sister Mary knuckle down.

Black, White, Yellow,
Red or Brown.

Stagecoach Mary
Mary Fields

Words and Music by:
Cecil Williams

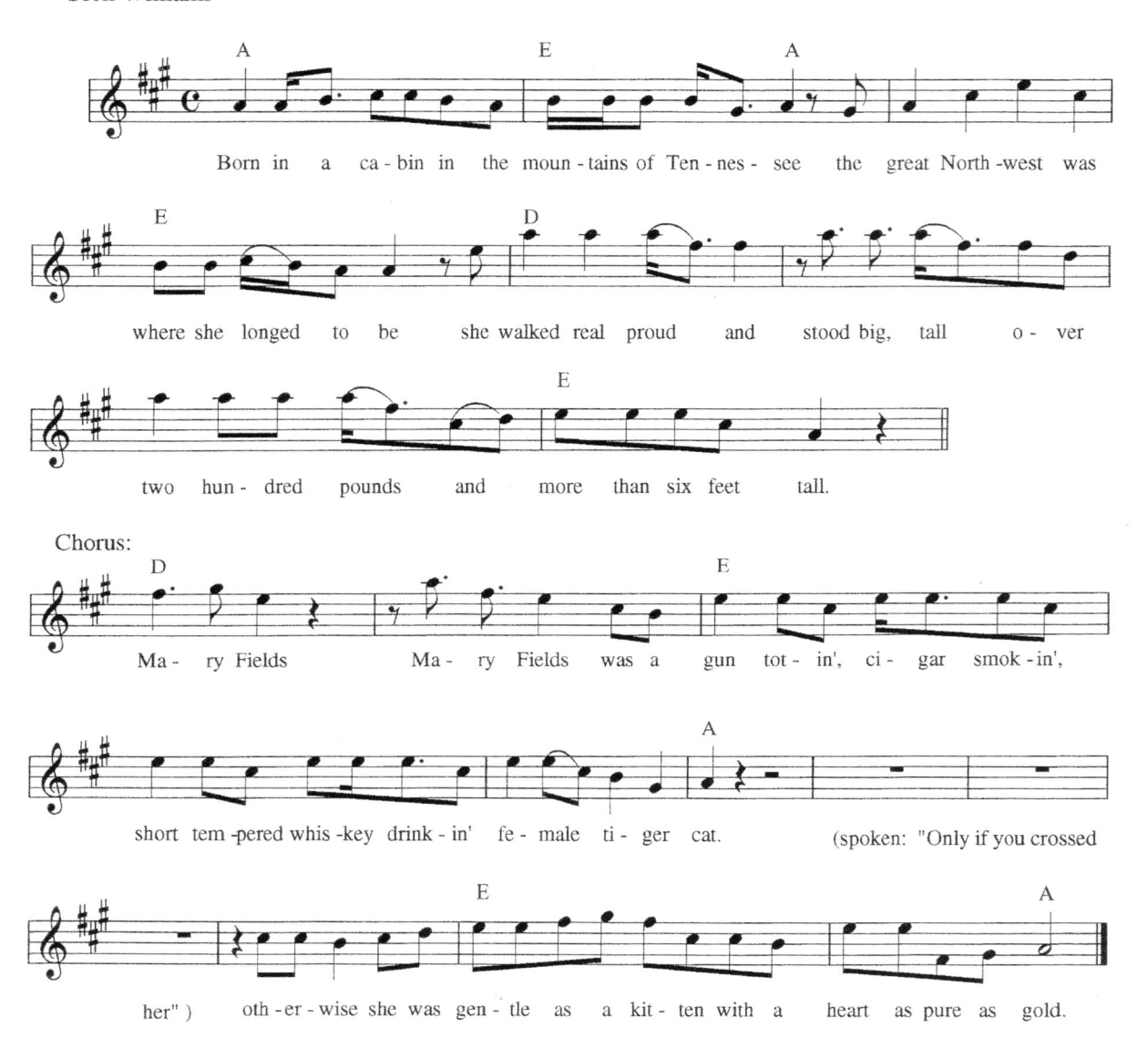

Born in a cabin in the mountains of Tennessee the great Northwest was where she longed to be she walked real proud and stood big, tall over two hundred pounds and more than six feet tall.

Chorus:

Mary Fields Mary Fields was a gun tot-in', cigar smok-in', short tem-pered whis-key drink-in' fe-male ti-ger cat. (spoken: "Only if you crossed her") oth-er-wise she was gen-tle as a kit-ten with a heart as pure as gold.

to next verse:

Copyright March 11, 1976   East Palo Alto, CA.

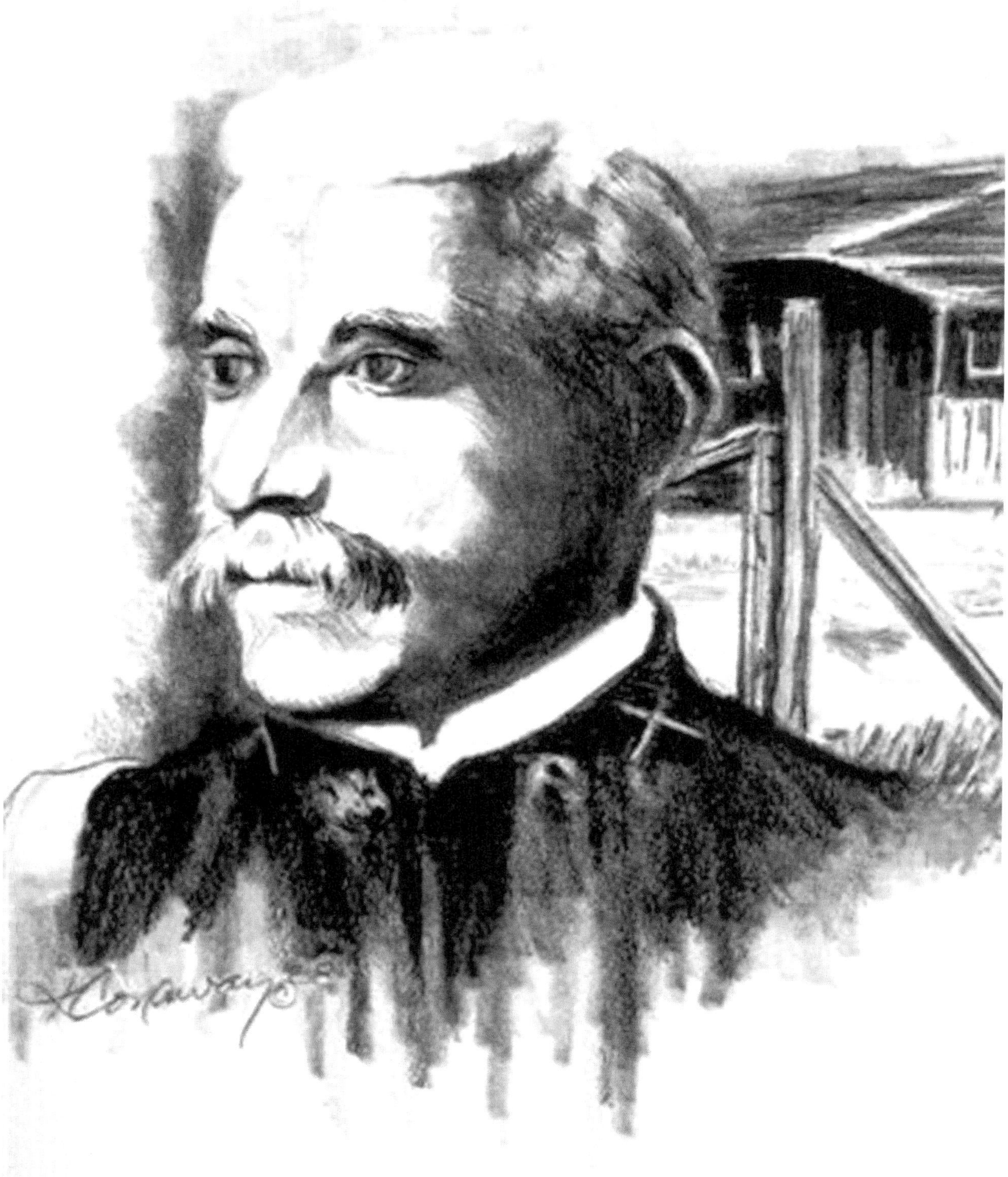

Lt. Henry Flipper and Colonel Allen Allensworth

Despite the fact that black soldiers had proved themselves in the Civil War and on the western frontier, the army continued to appoint white officers to command them until 1877. Then Henry O. Flipper became the first black to graduate from West Point. He was assigned to the Tenth Cavalry, one of the regiments the Indians had named the Buffalo Soldiers.

Flipper had endured the hazing and lack of friendship at West Point as one of three black cadets. At West Point the cadets "cloaked" him. For four years, every cadet ignored him and did not speak to him. Still he graduated fiftieth in a class of seventy-six. He served with distinction in the Tenth Cavalry in spite of white harassment until November, 1880.

On that date, he was charged with embezzling $3,791.77 from the post commissary, offering false testimony about the post accounts, and proposing to pay off the commissary deficit by writing a check on a bank where he had no account. He was found guilty of conduct unbecoming an officer and discharged. He was found not guilty of the more serious charge of embezzlement.

Flipper felt the charges had been brought because he had gone riding outside the fort with a white woman. Carroll states that a letter written by an officer of the Tenth indicates the charges were created falsely because Flipper had been "too familiar" in speaking to the wife of a white officer, who was a jealous southerner. (Carroll 349)

After his discharge, Flipper used the knowledge of Civil Engineering and Spanish he had acquired at West Point. His work in Mexico helped settle questions about land grants along the border and translate the mining laws of Mexico into English. He also made important contributions to international law, including his translation of the *Spanish and Mexican Land Laws*.

His outstanding work in translating and engineering caused him to be invited to join the National Geographic Society, Archaeological Institute of

The Black West in Story and Song

America, the Arizona Society of Civil Engineers, and other professional societies. During the Spanish-American War, several members of Congress supported his petition to be restored to his military rank. The Army turned his petition down on the basis that they were not recruiting black officers. The all black enlisted men and non-commissioned officers of Ninth and Tenth Cavalries and the Twenty-fourth and Twenty-fifth infantries fought in Cuba commanded by white officers.

After being refused his commission, he worked for mining companies in Mexico. Then he was appointed translator for the Senate subcommittee on Foreign Relations and served as an assistant to the Secretary of the Interior. He was rumored to have been a spy for the United States Punitive Expedition lead by General John J. Pershing against Pancho Villa in 1916. He always denied that he had any part in it.

When he died in 1940, his brother completed the death certificate question on his occupation by writing "Retired Army Officer." In 1999, long after his death, the United States Army recommended that dishonorable discharge be erased. In the written pardon and in the White House ceremony honoring Flipper, President Clinton recognized his service to his country both as an army officer and a civilian.

Allen Allensworth who had been born a slave on April 7, 1842, in Louisville, Kentucky, had more success in his military career than Henry Flipper did. When he was twelve, he was sold down the river for attempting to learn to read and write. He was sold on two other occasions before he successfully escaped.

First he served as a nurse with the United States Army. In 1863, he joined the United States Navy. He rose in rank from seaman to first class petty officer before he was honorably discharged April 4, 1865.

He worked as a civilian employee for the Navy at Mound City, Missouri, until 1867. Then he and his brother started two restaurants in St. Louis. Even though these were very successful financially, he longed to improve his education and enrolled at Eli Normal School. He sold his restaurants and became active teaching and preaching in churches in Missouri, Kentucky, and Ohio. In 1877 he married Josephine Leavell, a teacher, pianist, and organist in Louisville.

Town Founders, Townspeople, and Homesteaders:
Lt. Henry Flipper and Colonel Allen Allensworth

He learned in 1882 that the four black army regiments had only white chaplains. After being told that the chaplain for the Twenty-fourth infantry was retiring, he applied for the position. Until he applied the policy of the army was to appoint only white chaplains. In 1886, over the objections of many in the army, President Grover Cleveland appointed Allensworth to the rank of captain to serve as the chaplain for the Twenty-fourth regiment. Among the people recommending his appointment was one of his former owners, Mrs. A. P. Starbird.

Allensworth, who had been sold into the deep south for learning to read and write and who had finished his education as adult, now embarked on an attempt to bring education to the men of the Twenty-fourth. To the army's credit, it supported education for enlisted men and had a policy of educating the Buffalo Soldiers from their first formation. By 1889 it required all enlisted men to have the equivalent of an elementary education.

As an experienced, trained educator, Allensworth organized his school at Fort Bayard, New Mexico, carefully. He had a complete staff to teach the elementary grades, which had an enrollment of 118 in 1889. He separated his curriculum into two parts, one for children and one for soldiers.

For the soldiers each day of the week was devoted to a particular subject. His booklet, *Outline of Course of Study, and the Rules Governing Schools of Ft. Bayard, N. M.*, designates Monday for grammar, Tuesday for arithmetic, Wednesday for bookkeeping and writing, with the remainder of the week left for other basic subjects. His booklet also emphasizes the use of visual aids, which he usually had purchased from his pay. (Fowler 105)

His success as an educator of soldiers and the children of soldiers caused him to be invited to the National Education Association meeting in 1891 in Toronto. He requested permission to attend and deliver his paper, "Education in the United States Army." The army denied him permission to attend the meeting on the grounds that such orders were not covered in the regulations. This decision forced him to take a leave of absence and pay his own expenses to the convention. (Fowler 106)

Allensworth not only ministered to the educational and spiritual needs of the regiment, but he also attended to their social ones. He sponsored the literary and debating society that met once a week in the school. He encouraged the soldiers to read current events and made magazines, newspapers, and books available to all the soldiers whether they were enrolled in school or not.

Allensworth's work with the enlisted men did much to raise their morale and make them respected by the civilians they came in contact with. He and the other chaplains of the black regiments contributed a great deal to the army education program as it has developed today.

His contributions made him the first chaplain to receive the rank of Lieutenant Colonel. After he retired in 1906, he lectured throughout the East and Mid-west on the importance of education as a way to make Afro-Americans self-sufficient. Living in Los Angeles with his wife and two daughters, Allensworth joined with William Payne to put his ideas about self-sufficiency into practice. He and Payne, along with others, formed the California Colonization and Home Promotion Association to establish a black town on the Santa Fe line between Los Angeles and San Francisco. The association in recognition of his achievements named the town Allensworth.

While others busied themselves with governmental organization and civil problems, Allensworth, continuing his life-long commitment to education, made plans to establish a vocational school. Fresno and Tulare County legislators supported his plans. Nevertheless, many blacks and whites in California considered the idea of placing a state vocational school under black leadership as racist. The vocational school proposal was defeated. Tragically, in 1914, Colonel Allen Allensworth was killed when a motorcycle struck him.

After his death, the town continued to grow rapidly until a combination of factors caused its decline. Water problems caused by diversion projects, deep well pumping in surrounding areas, and demands for extensive irrigation slowed the productivity of the farms and the ranches the town depended upon. By World War II, more and more of the residents left the small town to enter industry in large cities. Those remaining tried new farming methods and businesses. In 1966, arsenic in large enough quantities to endanger public health was found in the water supply. This ended any hopes for the town.

Cornelius Ed Pope, who had grown up in Allensworth and worked for the California Department of Parks and Recreation in 1969, recognized the

Town Founders, Townspeople, and Homesteaders:
Lt. Henry Flipper and Colonel Allen Allensworth

potential of making the town into a preservation site for interpretive history to bring about the public awareness of the black experience in California. In 1976 the State Park and Recreation Commission voted to accept a plan to develop Colonel Allensworth State Historic Park, the first park in the United States named for a black man.

"Colonel Allensworth"

He was a scholar and a teacher, a Christian soldier man,
He loved his chosen people and did lend a helping hand.
He was a settler and a pioneer, his soul was in the land,
A dreamer and a builder of the trinity of man
I will share with you his story, I'll sing his bittersweet song
Of great pains and past glories mingles with a time long gone

(CHORUS)

Colonel Allensworth! Colonel Allensworth!
Your deeds must be remembered and your dreams held on high
Colonel Allensworth! Colonel Allensworth!
In your hearts your spirit lives and we pray will never die

The Golden West is where he settled and then formed a colony
A place to work and live together and raise a family
He was bought and sold as chattel in this land of liberty
Until that strong inner power said "My friend you must be free."
He escaped from chains of slavery and joined the freedom fight
Volunteered to serve his country doing what he felt was right
He felt the power of our Lord and the will to be free
A man must have a chance to be the best that he can be

(CHORUS)

In 1908 a town was founded, named in honor of their own
Allensworth, California, Allensworth, their new home
Yesterday has come and gone and his deeds still linger on
Tomorrow is another day, another dream they say,
There is a rumor going around, gonna change that little town
A new state park will be there for everyone to come and share
Betcha there'll be a little town square, a monument will be standing there.
Now folks come from far away to Allensworth, U. S. of A.

Colonel Allensworth! Colonel Allensworth!
In our hearts your spirit dwells, we trust and pray will never die

Colonel Allensworth

Words and Music by:
 Cecil Williams

He was a scho-lar and a teach-er a Chris-tian sol-dier man.

He loved his cho-sen peo-ple and did lend a help-ing hand.

He was a set-tler and a pio-neer. His soul was in the land.

A dream-er, and a build-er of the trin-i-ty of man.

Chorus:

Col-onel Al-lens-worth, Al-len Al-lens-worth,

Your deeds must be re-mem-bered and your dreams held on high.

Col-onel Al-len Al-lens-worth, Al-len Al-lens-worth,

in our hearts your spir-it lives and we pray will ne-ver die.

Copyright July 12, 1976   East Palo Alto, CA.   to next verse:

157

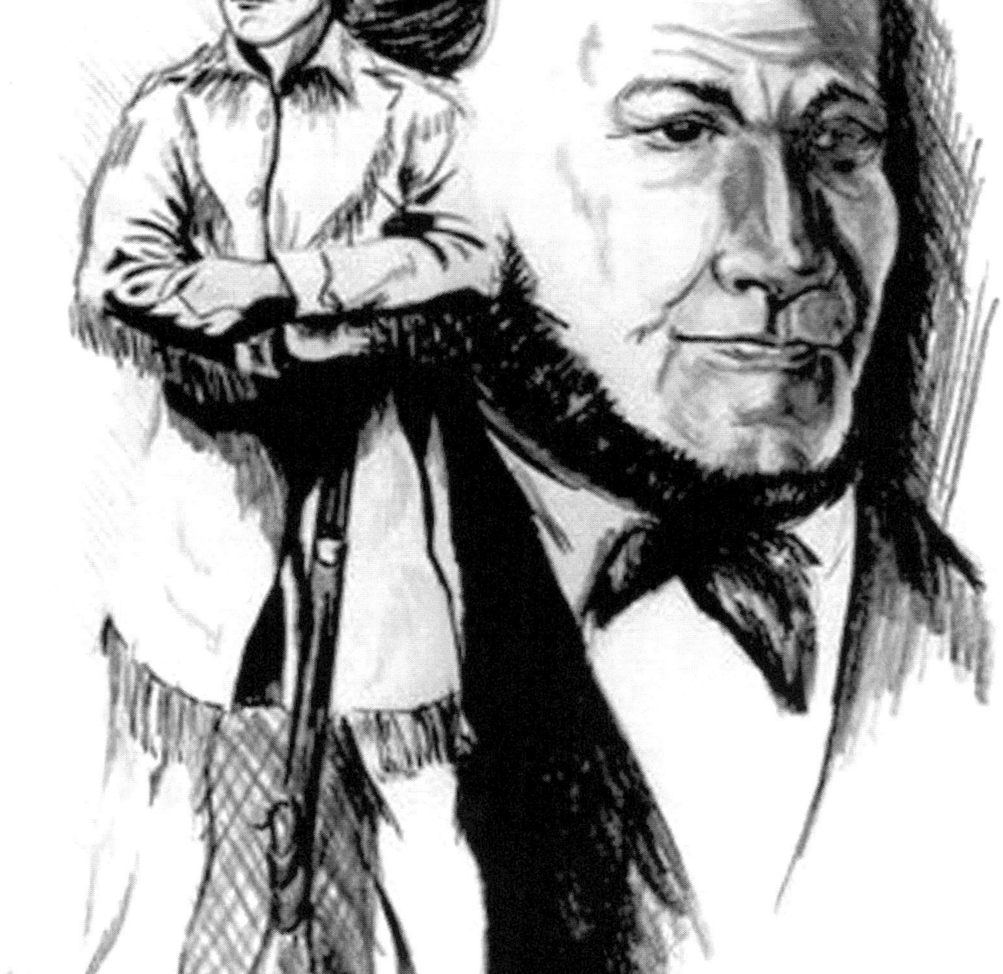

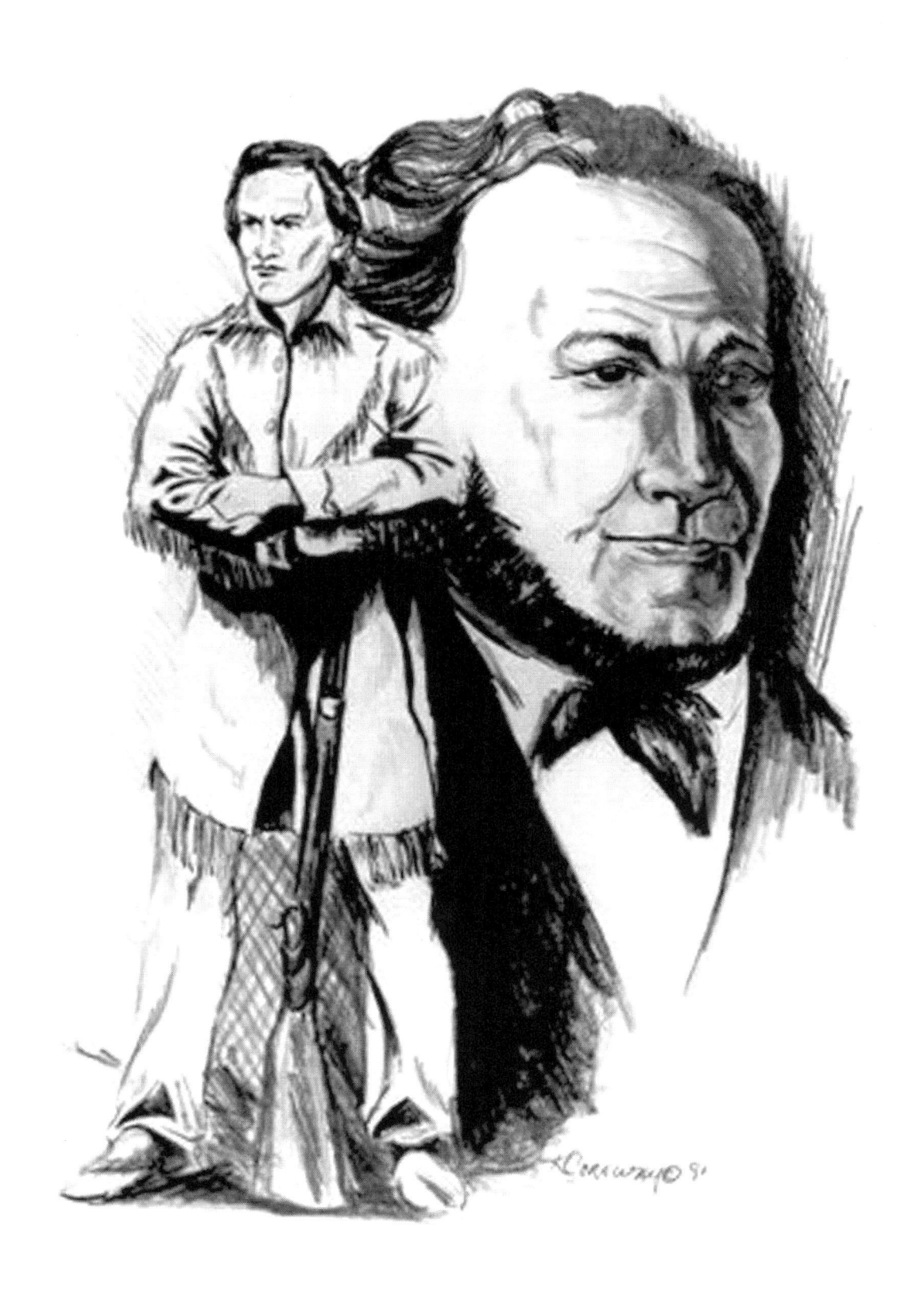

George Washington Bush

Michael T. Simmons, an Irish immigrant, and the white homesteaders who traveled with him in 1844 to the Columbia River Valley had agreed that they would not settle in any place that did not extend equal rights to their friend and leader, George Washington Bush, a black. They had heard that any black man who settled in Oregon would be whipped and driven out of the territory. As a group they vowed to fight to protect him.

Bush had fought with Andrew Jackson at the Battle of New Orleans and had made a good deal of money in the cattle business in Missouri. He had married a white woman, had five children, bought a farm, and had begun to think of Missouri as his permanent home.

But Missouri had passed a law in 1844 banning free blacks from the state, forcing Bush to seek freedom from prejudice and discrimination in the West. He told his friend John Minto about his decision to immigrate:

In Missouri I was a wealthy man. I had a big farm and a large herd of cattle. But life is not easy for a man with dark skin, not even a wealthy man with an educated white wife like Isabelle. We hoped that far away, on the frontier, we might finally find peace (Pelz, 15).

The Oregon legislature had passed a law prohibiting black settlers in the territory, so Bush and his party decided to settle in the part of the territory still claimed by England. Before the wagon train led by Bush and Simmons reached the Oregon border, they knew that they were going to defy the British ban against Americans settling in the Puget Sound region. The British wanted the region free of American settlers to reserve it for the monarch and the Hudson's Bay Fur Company. Nevertheless, the Bush-Simmons party broke the law and started homesteading there, becoming the first Americans to settle north of the Columbia River.

In leading the party from St. Joseph, Missouri, to the Northwest, Bush had financially supported at least two families and provided excellent leadership. He was the only member of the party familiar with the West because he had been a fur trapper there in his early days with Joseph Robidoux. His advice was always brief and practical. "Boys, you are going through hard country. You have the guns and ammunition. Take my advice: anything you see as big as a blackbird, kill and eat it" (Katz 76). All who made the trip on the Oregon Trail remember him as a generous leader they admired.

Two years after the Bush-Simmons party had settled in British territory, the United States and England settled their Oregon boundary dispute. This settlement offered new problems for the homesteaders who had come with Bush even though the successful American claim to the region was based on their land claims. Bush had long ago determined that if he could not have a free man's rights in the United States, he would settle in Mexico. Now he was under the control of Oregon laws, which prohibited blacks from settling there.

To overcome this, Simmons, who had been elected to the Oregon legislature in 1854, sponsored a bill exempting Bush and his family from these discriminatory laws. He petitioned the United States Congress to grant Bush a homestead. The bill to exempt the Bush family passed. Congress in 1855 granted Bush a 640-acre tract, which is known today as Bush Prairie.

With their rights guaranteed, the Bush family quickly became known throughout the territory for their generosity. They aided new homesteaders and shared their crops with the needy, simply saying to each and all, black or white, "Return it when you can."

In 1852, the grain supplies became quite low that winter on Puget Sound. Prices were rising rapidly because speculators were trying to buy the entire crop. Speculators rode out to Bush Prairie and attempted to buy his wheat crop. George Bush said, "I'll keep my grain, so that my neighbors will have enough to live on and for seeding their fields in the spring. They have no money to pay your fancy prices, and I don't intend to see them want for anything I can provide them with" (Katz 77). This incident epitomizes Bush's attitude toward his friends, neighbors, and life.

Town Founders, Townspeople, and Homesteaders: *George Washington Bush*

Additionally, he was quite interested in new farming developments. He was the first to have a sawmill, gristmill, mower, and reaper in the region. While he was interested in modern farming methods, he also was able to maintain good relations with the Indians because of his amiability and his belief in fair play.

He died in 1863 before he could see all black people emancipated. However, his sons carried on the way of life he had established by developing their farming skills, helping their neighbors and being politically active. Their crops often were winners at local and country fairs. The wheat crop of one of the sons was exhibited at the Smithsonian in Washington, D.C. Another son, William Owen Bush, served two terms in the legislature, a legislature that had barred black settlers from Oregon earlier.

Porter calls George Bush, "...a leader of in the first significant American settlement north of the Columbia..." (363). His influence through his generosity and his sons extends down to the present day as a model life. He was a man who believed in individual freedom, but was always ready to help his fellow man.

"54-40 Or Fight"

When we laid claim to the Puget Sound
No shots were fired, not a single round,
The state of Washington might not have been
Without the loyalty of two friends.

   (CHORUS)

Bush and Simmons, together they stood,
Fighting the odds as best they could.

Cussin' the Union Jack and the Stars and Stripes
An immigrant, Irish, and a man, half-white,
Now that treaty was signed in 1844
But the saga began years before.
One sought freedom from across the sea,
The other fought to be free.
   (CHORUS)

Bush was a man of valor and deed.
Was not a slave, and yet not free.
He fought with Jackson in New Orleans
For liberty, justice and the American Dream
Freedom for all did not mean
All were free to be free men.
   (CHORUS)

So hitching up and westward ho!
Across the Oregon Trail they did go.
The Oregon Trail brought hard times,
But the biggest challenge was the color line.
No blacks can enter, that's the law of the land,
So be the law, but together we stand.
   (CHORUS)

They crossed the Columbia and settled down
In and around the Puget Sound.
So when Polk challenged that ol' Union Jack,
It was based upon one white and one black.
54-40 or fight echoed the world around
And yet few really knew what went down.
   (CHORUS)

So Michael Simmons and George Washington Bush,
Good friends, loyal and true.
We appreciate what you stand for,
And we salute the both of you.

54 - 40 or Fight
George Washington Bush

Words and Music by:
Cecil Williams

When we laid claim to the Puget Sound no shots were fired, not a single round. The state of Washington might not have been without the loyalty of two friends.

Chorus:

Bush and Simmons together they stood fighting the odds as best they could.

to next verse:

Copyright November 14, 1990 Rolla, MO.

Bibliography

The Black West in Story and Song

Adams, Russell L. *Great Negroes Past and Present.* Chicago: Afro-Am. Press, 1964.

Ambrose, Stephen E. *Undaunted Courage: Meriwether Lewis, Thomas Jefferson, and the Opening of the American West.* New York: Simon and Schuster, 1996.

Aptheker, Herbert (ed.) *A Documentary History of the Negro People in the United States.* New York: Citadel, 1951.

Athearn, Robert G. *In Search of Canaan: Black Migration to Kansas 1879-80.* Lawrence: The Regents Press of Kansas, 1978.

Berwanger, Eugene. *The Frontier Against Slavery.* Urbana: University of Illinois Press, 1967.

Betts, Robert B.(With New Epilogue by James J. Holmberg.) *The Search for York: The Slave Who Went to the Pacific with Lewis and Clark.* Boulder, CO.: University of Colorado Press, 2000.

Blumberg, Rhoda. *York's Adventures with Lewis and Clark: The African-American's Part in the Great Expedition.* New York: Harper Collins, 2004.

Bonner, T. D. (ed.) *The Life and Adventures of James P. Beckwourth.* New York: Arno Press, 1969.

Bontemps, Arna and Jack Conroy. *Anyplace But Here.* New York: Hill and Wang, 1968.

Cashin, Herschel V., et al. *Under Fire with the Tenth U. S. Cavalry.* New York: Arno Press, 1969.

Cornish, Dudley Taylor. *The Sable Arm.* New York: Norton, 1966.

Downey, Fairfax. *Indian-Fighting Army.* New York: Bantam Books, 1957.

Drotning, Philip T. *Black Heroes in Our Nation's History: A Tribute to Those Who Helped Shape America.* New York: Cowles Book Co., 1969.

____. *A Guide to Negro History in America.* New York: Doubleday, 1968.

Durham, Philip and Everett L. Jones. *The Negro Cowboys.* New York: Dodd, Mean, 1965.

Fletcher, Marvin. *The Black Soldier and Officer in the United States Army, 1891-1917.* Columbia: University of Missouri Press, 1974.

Flipper, Henry Ossian. *The Colored Cadet at West Point.* New York: Arno Press, 1968.

Franklin, John Hope. *From Slavery to Freedom.* New York: Knopf, 1967.

Gibbs, Mifflin W. *Shadow and Light.* New York: Arno Press, 1968.

Gugliotta, Bobette. *Nolle Smith: Cowboy, Engineer, Statesman.* New York: Dodd, Mead and Co., 1971.

Haley, James Evetts. *Charles Goodnight: Cowman and Plainsman.* Norman: University of Oklahoma Press, 1949.

Hill, Mozell C. "The All-Negro Communities of Oklahoma: The Natural History of a Social Movement." *Journal of Negro History* 31 (July 1946) 254-268.

Holmberg, James J. *Dear Brother: Letters of William Clark to Jonathan Clark.* New Haven, Conn.: Yale University Press, 2002.

____. *Exploring with Lewis and Clark: The 1804 Journal of Charles Floyd.* Norman: University of Oklahoma Press, 2005.

Hughes, Langston. *Famous Negro Heroes of America.* New York: Dodd, Mead and Co., 1965.

Johnson, Jalmar. *Builders of the Northwest.* New York: Dodd, Mead, 1966.

Katz, William Loren. *The Black West.* Seattle, WA: Open Hand Publishing, 1987.

____. *Black Indians: A Hidden Heritage.* New York: Atheneum, 1986.

____. *The Black West.* New York: Doubleday and Co., 1971.

____. *Eyewitness: The Negro in American History.* New York: Pitman Publishing, 1967.

Lamprugh, George R. "The Image of the Negro in Popular Magazine Fiction, 1875-1900." *Journal of Negro History* 56 (April 1972) 177-188.

Lapp, Rudolph M. "The Negro in Gold Rush California." *Journal of Negro History* 49 (April 1964).

Leckie, William H. *The Buffalo Soldiers.* Norman: University of Oklahoma Press, 1967.

Lee, Irvin H. *Negro Medal of Honor Men.* New York: Dodd, Mead, 1967.

Lindenmeyer, Otto. *Black and Brave.* New York: McGraw-Hill, 1970.

____. *Black History: Lost, Strayed or Stolen.* New York: Avon, 1979.

Love, Nat. *The Life and Adventures of Nat Love Better Known in the Cattle Country as "Deadwood Dick" by Himself.* New York: Arno Press, 1968.

Millis, Walter. *The Martial Spirit.* Boston: Little, Brown, 1931.

Mundis, Jerrold J. "He Took the Bull by the Horns." *American Heritage* 19 (December 1967) 50-55.

Painter, Nell Irvin. *Exodusters.* New York: Knopf, 1976.

Porter, Kenneth W. *The Negro on the American Frontier.* New York: Arno Press, 1971.

____. "Negro Labor in the Western Cattle Industry." *Labor History* 10 (Summer 1969) 346-374.

Quarles, Benjamin. *The Negro in the Civil War.* New York: De Capo Press, 1989.

Remington, Frederic. *Frederic Remington's Own West.* New York: Dial Press, 1960.

Rickey, Don Jr. *Forty Miles a Day on Bread and Beans, the Enlisted Soldier Fighting the Indian Wars.* Norman: University of Oklahoma Press, 1963.

Siringo, Charles. *A Texas Cow Boy: or Fifteen Years on the Hurricane Deck of a Spanish Pony.* Chicago: M. Umbdendstock, 1885.

Savage, W. Sherman. "The Negro in the Westward Movement." *Journal of Negro History* 25 (October 1940) 531-539.

____. *Blacks in the West.* Westport, CT: Greenwood Press, 1976.

Thompson, Erwin N. "The Negro Soldiers on the Frontier: A Fort Davis Case Study." *Journal of the West* 7 (April 1968) 217-235.

Van Deusen, John G. "The Exodus of 1879." *Journal of Negro History* 21 (October 1936) 111-129.

Voegeli, V. Jacque. *Free but Not Equal.* Chicago: University of Chicago Press, 1967.

Wallace, Edward S. "General John Lapham Bullis, Thunderbolt of Texas Frontier." *Southwestern Historical Quarterly* 40 (July 1951) 77-85.

The Black West in Story and Song

Wright, Richard. "Negro Companions of the Spanish Explorers." In August Meir and Elliott M. Rudwick (eds.) *The Making of Black America*, Vol. I. New York: Atheneum, 1969.

Biographical Sketch

Cecil Williams

Cecil Williams was educated in segregated schools. He completed elementary grades in Fairfax, Oklahoma. He had to go to high school in Pawhuska, Oklahoma, 30 miles from home, because there was no high school for Blacks in Fairfax. He graduated from Langston University in Oklahoma.

At an early age, Cecil saw the need to do extensive research to find and fill in the left-out contributions of Blacks in settling the West.

As a cartographer, he began writing ballads as a hobby, leading to concerts all across the United States and Lagos, Nigeria. His motto is always to enlighten, inform, entertain, and inspire.

He has written 58 ballads and is still writing. He is a member of the Missouri Folklore Society, the Oklahoma Historical Society and co-founder of The Lincoln Colored School Museum Society, which was placed on the National and Oklahoma State Register in 2003.

Cecil and his wife are retired and live on a farm in Rolla, Missouri. Anyone who would like to buy a tape or cd of Cecil's songs may write him at 14661 State Route F or call him at: 573-341-3856.

Biographical Sketch

Keith Conaway

Keith Conaway was born in Lexington, Missouri, and grew up in Kansas City. After graduating from Central High School there, he enrolled at the University of Missouri-Rolla, where he graduated in 1981 with a degree in Engineering Management.

Throughout his life, his primary interest has been in art, however. He is a self-taught artist who founded a design and drawing company, doing graphic art and commissioned portraits. He has also done religious murals for several churches. More recently he has executed a series of pen and ink drawings of the major figures in black history.

He lives in Rolla with his wife Gladys and his two children, William and Syrhea.

Keith has available T-shirts and drawings of the Black West. His mailing address is 9 Dogwood Lane, Rolla, MO 65401, and his website is theblackwest3000@Yahoo.com

Biographical Sketch of Michael Patrick

Photo courtesy of Diane Ehlers

Michael Patrick was born at Lake Ozark, Missouri, and attended Eldon Public Schools, where he was graduated from high school in 1952. He received a B.S. in 1956 and an M.A. in 1957 from Southern Illinois University-Carbondale. He taught as an instructor at the University of Missouri-Columbia where he received his Ph. D. in 1966. He became an assistant professor at Western Kentucky University. He then taught at the University of Missouri-Rolla from 1966-92. He retired in 1992 and became Emeritus Professor.

He has been active in the Missouri Folklore Society and has served two terms as president of that organization. He has also been president of the Ozark States Folklore Society. In 1989, he was named a fellow in the Institute for the Study of the Southern Novel at the University of North Carolina.

He has published articles on Romantic and Victorian poetry, the contemporary novel, and folklore in a variety of journals including *Romantic Reassessment, Costerus Essays, The Wordsworth Circle*, the *Missouri Folklore Journal*, and *The Journal of North American Culture*.

His book, *We Are a Part of History: The Story of the Orphan Trains*, written in collaboration with Evelyn Sheets and Evelyn Trickel, was published by Lightning Tree Press, Santa Fe, New Mexico, in 1991. Donning Press republished it in 1995, and it is still in print. His second book, *Orphan Trains to Missouri*, written with Evelyn Trickel, was published by the University of Missouri Press in 1997 and also is still in print.

Since 1995 he has lived in Fairhope, Alabama.